I0451556

SCARLET SPOTLIGHT

J.X. Burros

JX Stories and Media

ISBN-13: 978-0-9852453-7-5

Cover design by: Jeffrey Guntly
Library of Congress Control Number: 2018675309
Printed in the United States of America

To my mother, my first faithful reader

CONTENTS

PROLOGUE

"Alright, are you guys ready?" A moderately high-pitched, slightly nasally male voice asked from somewhere close, but unseen by the camera. Tom was the strict director—the mastermind, of sorts. He held the camera very steady and centered, making sure to capture the scene in the best light.

The embraced couple in view giggled. They lay on top of each other, like they were enjoying the day alone. The guy on screen, Jack, was obviously a sports guy. He was tall, with sun-grazed skin, and sandy blond, ruffled hair. While masculine in appearance, he was plainly not into manhood quite yet. His muscles were visible, protruding from his basketball jersey, but they weren't quite as defined as they could be. They were slightly surrounded by the baby fat he would lose in a year or two. His facial hair didn't grow in visibly yet, but that never stopped him from trying to grow it out. The white-colored fur stuck out above his lip and below his chin, only showing flashes in the right angle of light. He barely looked at the camera when he said, in a rough, playful voice, "Of course. I was born to tap this piece of ass." He added a soft growl in the girl's ear.

Hannah looked as a stereotypically beautiful young woman would. Her long, platinum hair sprawled beneath her on the couch like a spot of water on a countertop. Her perfectly glistening white skin was soft and flawless, her entire slender frame visible in a very revealing cheerleader's uniform. She smiled, showing off dazzlingly white teeth, and continued to giggle, staring at Jack with stars in her bright blue eyes as he continued to grind himself on top of her.

The scene was set. The walls of the room were bare, showing off the less-than-eye-catching light brown color. The couch was cheap, but intact and a slightly darker shade of the wall's. Everything about the small, bare living room would draw the eye directly to the middle at the teenage couple.

"Alright, then—Action!" the hidden voice yelled as the camera began to roll. After a bit of silence, he continued, "Say the line!" His voice sounded a bit more annoyed.

"Don't worry, baby," Jack started. "I won't hurt you." He kept his muddy eyes locked on Hannah as he stroked her soft, rosy cheek.

Hannah put her finger on his chest. She bit her lip, slowly trailing her hand down to the bottom of his jersey and began to gradually pull it off. It was like they'd done it a thousand times. The shirt never caught on Jack's chin, as was common in amateur adult media. As soon as the shirt was free of his face, Jack put his lips onto hers and thrust his hands under her tight shirt. He wrenched it off with a hungry intensity.

The camera moved closer to the action. "Keep going," Tom yelled over them, though they obviously would've anyway, "but you two should try to keep a similar pace with each other!"

"...been waiting for so long to be able to do this," Jack continued as he straightened up, the curves of his young muscles casting faint shadows on his body. His hands felt the length of her arms to her fingertips, then back to her shoulders, redirecting down her chest, tracing the bottom line of her bra, then down to her bare stomach.

"Oh!" Hannah squealed as Jack's hands found a sensitive spot at the edge of her skirt. She squirmed under his touch, but he pinned her down. She threw her arms around his neck and pulled his lips back to hers. Soon enough, what was a hard pressing of lips became a hungry, driven exploration of mouths, signaling Hannah's hand to move down the contours of Jack's side, to the top of his shorts. She followed the end of it for a second before pulling it down just half an inch.

"Are you ready?" Jack asked breathily, breaking off the kiss.

Hannah got close to Jack's ear and whispered, attempting to be loud enough for the camera, but still sensually quiet, "I was always ready."

"Hannah!" Tom directed. "Kiss right below

3

his ear on his neck!"

She followed the orders fluidly, as if Tom's voice was simply her own subconscious. Her face buried itself inside the grove of his head and shoulder. Jack's eyes closed as he tilted his head up, letting a soft, low moan escape from his mouth. He remained frozen, smiling idiotically, but completely oblivious.

Hannah left her lips there for more than a few seconds. It almost became awkwardly silent as Jack's grinding hips slowed their pace. The momentum faded until there was a loud yelp coming from Jack.

Tom yelled, "Hey, what's going on?"

Jack jumped off of Hannah, his hand flying instantly to the spot where her lips had been seconds before. He stared at her then pulled his hand to his face to look at it. It was filthy red and dripping with blood. He shared his gaze between the mess and Hannah until he locked onto her with furious eyes. "You little bitch!" he growled.

He lunged at her, as the cameraman backed away, still locked on the scene gone awry. As if by magic, she flew off of the couch, off-screen, in a split-second. Jack crashed onto the fabric, bumbling away the decorative pillows and throwing them to the floor. She returned back in a flash as Jack stood up, but swiftly kicked him in the stomach, causing him to double over on the floor. What had once been a carefree, innocent smile moments ago had become overtaken by something darker, more malicious. The arches of her eyebrows pulled themselves downward in the middle, separating two cold, calculating eyes. The muscles in her face curved her smile higher, revealing whiter and sharper teeth. Her breaths were longer and deeper as she stared at the huffing mess on the floor. Jack reached his hand outwards, to nowhere in particular, trying to steady himself. Hannah took it, yanked it closer and used her other hand to plunge deep into his skull.

The frame jerked as the impact caused a horrible scream from the boy before he slumped over, dead. The camera sat still, Tom's breathing increasing as he sat, and watching Hannah as the blood seeped into the carpet.

Suddenly, her head snapped in the direction of the camera. The cold grin still took hold of Hannah's face. Immediately, the cameraman dove to the right, directly into a window. He broke right through it, tumbling through a spray of glass and pain with a malicious vixen jumping right after.

The man and the camera smashed to the ground, surrounded by shattered, bloodied glass. The camera tumbled away, out of Tom's reach, but feed was unharmed, pointed straight at him, lying on the ground. His instinct was to move, and it showed clearly on his pale face, but within less than a second, Hannah was on top of him, pinning him down with no way to escape. Her cold skin sparkled in the sunlight, and it was obvious that he was finished.

She stared down at him with a hunger in her eyes. It was something dead, something cold, yet it was something sexual, alluring. It was something the human brain couldn't possibly comprehend. But she didn't strike. She slowed and began to breathe deeply. Her face turned to horror as she stared at her bare skin. Rapidly, the once ice-cold skin was quickly turning shades of darker and darker red, as if she was getting sunburned at one-hundred times the speed. The monster once called Hannah screamed and her body went through what one could only call rapid decomposition. The skin darkened at an increasing pace until the skin pulled itself together, tightening over her bones. Within seconds, the only thing left was a dark mangled corpse sprawled on the porcelain white snow.

Tom panted heavily, unbelievably alive, and turned to his right at the camera. His long, curly hair was now a mix of his natural brown, a dark blood-infested red, and blackened flesh. His glasses were strewn and broken, and his lip was bleeding. He didn't move. His small frame simply grew and deflated with every gasping, coughing breath, treasuring every intake of air like it was his last.

CHAPTER ONE

I turned around in my black, ratted swivel chair to face my team with a huge smile on my face. They had found space in my cramped, messy room to sit on the floor. "So," I asked, "how is it?"

Their looks of awe slowly turned into smiles as they began to high five.

"That's amazing!" Hannah exclaimed. "I actually had to look down at my arms—just to make sure that didn't really happen!" I noticed her touch her arm a little uncomfortably. She looked almost the same as she did in the video —minus the malicious look in her eyes and the decomposition of her skin.

"Dude," Jack remarked, "does the inside of me really look like that?" Jack had a way pointing out things like that. Paired with his monotone voice, he often sounded like a frequent pot smoker. He wasn't, but there was always speculation.

We all chattered nonsensically for a few minutes until I finally quieted them down. "Okay, okay," I said. "So, is it real?"

They looked at me oddly for a second. "Um, no," stated Hannah. "If it was real, we wouldn't have spent weeks getting the filming right, spending countless hours throwing broken glass in the air, combing through tons of movie cuts, and losing sleep to editing all-nighters." She and Jack started a round of laughter. Alicia stayed stoic.

Alicia was the last of our group. She refused to be a part of the camera—which was fine since there weren't any more parts, but she was an odd sort of girl—a hot sort of odd girl. She was smart, and got straight A's I'm pretty sure, but she wasn't timid or shy like most nerds. She never grasped at the edges for attention, but she always got it. She may have been a bitch sometimes, but she was gorgeous and intelligent. Honestly, those were the only two things I could imagine that would keep her string tethered to my heart. She could probably have the entire school around her finger, but for whatever reason, the tall, soft-skinned, immaculately dressed, perfectly colored Asian girl chose to waste her free time with me. I was perfectly okay with that.

"That's not what I meant," I said, rolling my eyes. "Plus, I did almost all of that work...except for the file-combing. Alicia did that."

"And a damn good job of it, too!" Alicia snapped.

"True, true," I admitted, nodding my head. "However, does it look real?"

They all went silent for a few moments. They awkwardly looked at each other. "It was great—" Jack started slowly, knowing that he should pick his words carefully.

I quickly cut him off, "Spare my feelings. I need the truth. What's wrong with it? What was unbelievable?" We needed this to work. I needed this to work.

"Besides the vampire?" Jack bravely said. "The sexy, sexy vampire." He looked at Hannah mischievously, as he always did. He followed it by trying to get his hand up her skirt.

She slapped his hand. "Or that this bastard could get in my pants?" Hannah countered. He mocked an offended look, but Hannah just smiled at him and looked back at me.

"Yes," I groaned, "besides that." I stifled my laughter at their antics, trying to keep the topic on track. Even though there was really not set time frame for the project, my heart was beating faster, telling me to hurry.

They continued an awkward silence. They looked at each other and mumbled little bits of nothing that were entirely unproductive. I sighed and rolled my eyes again. I spun my chair back to the computer screen. I restarted the file and told them, "This time, look for flaws."

They all stared intensely at the screen. I looked at it myself, for the millionth time. I knew there was something off. I needed to believe it myself. I wanted the hair of my arms to stand on end. I wanted feel the need to run my fingers to be sure that there was no blood caked inside.

When it finished, I stared them down

expectantly.

"The first...uh, blood-thingy, is a little choppy," Jack piped up. I had noticed that a bit, and if Jack did, too, everyone else in the world would.

After a few minutes longer, Hannah said, "You need to get my skin to sparkle the second it hits sunlight." I thought I had the timing down right, but apparently not.

"How about the decomposition?" I asked. I wasn't so familiar with that part, and I needed to know if Average Joe would believe it.

"That part is perfect," Alicia spoke again. I felt a little blood rush to my cheeks when she complimented me. Alicia had a little effect over me. My little schoolboy crush on her took hold of my tongue.

"Yeah," Hannah added.

I regained the use of my words and turned to Alicia. "Come on, Alicia, you're the mean one..." Alicia gave me a filthy look. "Sorry, critical one," I corrected. "I know you have more critical things to say."

Plainly, she said, "Lower the quality."

"Of course!" I exclaimed. It all made sense. It looked like a movie—a Hollywood movie, if I might say. It looked too good. We needed it too look like we kids got together to be horny teenagers with my dad's camera and ended up with the footage of the century.

I turned back to the computer instantly. Before I could click on anything, Jack yelled out,

"Stop!" I jumped and looked at him. He continued, "Save a copy and change that one."

I paused. "Why?"

"Well," he said awkwardly, "the original just looks so cool."

"What are we going to do with it?" I inquired, impatient.

He shrugged. I obliged, emphasizing every click immaturely. I could hear Hannah chastising Jack behind me, as well as a soft "What?" in Jack's voice. I paid them no mind. I began to tweak the video a little more, losing myself in the settings and changes, cuttings and effects. The three of them conversed together behind me, but I couldn't hear a word. I focused myself entirely into this project. This was our future—*my* future. It wasn't long before the group began to disband. I wouldn't have even noticed had Hannah not left first, giving me a hug on my shoulders before she walked out. I only turned my head to say goodbye to her. Alicia left minutes after that, simply getting up and leaving. I turned around in my chair to tell her goodbye, but she'd already made it to the door.

Jack was the only one left. We were always together. There were always laughs and high fives going around. The only thing I could gather that made us so inseparable was time. We had been together for so long that it seemed weird not to. He was a grade-A jock: football, basketball, and golf. He hung out with all of the popular kids, skated by in school, and high-fived at the glimpse of a cheerleader's ass. I wasn't. I was pretty much a loner. The video group was my only set of friends —not that I needed any more.

I saved the file on my computer and collapsed onto my bed. I groaned.

Jack, moving comfortably in my bean bag chair, asked, "What?"

"So much work..." I replied with an exhausted voice.

He sat up. "Hey," he said, "no one is making you do this. This is all your own."

"True," I responded, "but it's too late to abandon it now. Plus, you guys would hate me."

"You're damn right we would," he confirmed.

We simply laughed for a second. It was incredibly monotonous, but there was comfort in repetition.

"So," he broke, "do you think I have another shot with Hannah?"

"Oh, Jesus Christ," I replied. "How many times have you gone out? Five? Six?"

"Four," he clarified. "Plus, three of those, *she* broke up with *me*."

"Then, why does she keep going out with you?" He shrugged his shoulders. "Don't you think she'll get bored of you?" He rolled his eyes. "Ugh, women," I remarked, not actually thinking about Jack's situation, but my own—not that it really actually existed, anyway. Alicia was almost like a celebrity in my mind. I could watch her from a distance, but I couldn't touch her—at least, not without getting smacked. We'd been out once, but it was like watching a movie. I didn't even remember most of it, but I was faintly told the story. I didn't know how the characters felt, but it was one of the best stories I'd ever heard.

"You've got that right," he agreed, and it faintly tapped me out of my misery.

I continued to lie on the bed, trying to fully recover, but my problems drew me back in, pulling me deeper and deeper.

It wasn't until Jack spoke up that I finally snapped up. "Wanna play CoD?"

I nodded in agreement. Senseless violence, separate from reality, was a perfect way to get me out of my own head. I fired up the system connected to my small, fuzzy screen, and listened to the machine purr. Well, it was more of a growl. I'd bought a used system for much cheaper, but it made a lot of peculiar noises. Regardless, it did its job.

The sound effects of the game crackled as it started, but I paid it no mind. Jack had played with my subpar equipment before, and I was sure he already knew the kinks in it. The game came to life, and I dove headfirst into it. Surrounded by guns and blood, my mind melted, registering only the objective at hand.

I never fully understood why I felt that this was a real social situation, we barely said any words to each other, but amidst the gunfire and bellowing at the screen, it was peaceful.

I was on a whole other planet an hour later. Jack and I weren't merely friends; we were teammates, holding each other's backs. I didn't even budge when I faintly heard Jack's phone buzz.

"Alright," Jack said as he got up, "well, I gotta get going. I'm meeting this chick at the burger place." He threw the controller onto the bed without pausing or anything, leaving me alone.

"'Kay, bye," I said without getting up. I smashed the buttons furiously until I ultimately died twenty seconds later. I could've made a snide comment, but it didn't surprise me that he was going out with some other chick, even though he was desperately in love with Hannah. He was a player. Everyone knew it. I'm not sure why these girls kept going out with him, especially Hannah. He was just cool, I guess. Or it was the fact that all of the girls thought he was incredibly gorgeous. Girls never made any sense.

The door shut and I could hear the rumble of the engine as Jack left. Then, it was only me. I sat there, starting another game, but it was over before I knew it. I turned the system off in a huff and collapsed back onto my bed, letting the dark clouds surround my consciousness.

I foolishly had thought that this was the last night before we could plan the send. I didn't even have the energy to get out of my bed. I knew I should, but my thoughts kept crashing into me like waves—their hands grabbing at me, pulling me under. They wrenched at my body continuously, desperately taking me to the deepest trenches of the ocean…

…but that damn beeping wouldn't end. I thrust my arm out to find my alarm clock, but missed. No table, no clock, no empty pop cans. I thrust my eyes open, cringing to the sunlight. I had fallen asleep right after Jack left, and now my muscles were sore from sleeping incorrectly.

I pulled myself to the other side of the bed, and fought my way through clutter to reach the alarm clock. I pressed "snooze" and collapsed into my bed for five minutes before the beeping started up again. At that point, I turned it off. I'd had enough sleep. I threw myself to the floor in an attempt to wake up.

I pulled on some clothes that seemed clean, and slugged out of the room. Upon standing up, it didn't feel like I'd been sleeping so long. I assumed that all of those two o'clock nights finally decided to catch up with me—when I finally got a full night of sleep.

I grabbed my keys, and pretty soon, I was at school, in class. I didn't remember the drive, or getting out of the car, or even sitting down in my seat, but eventually, I was there. There were little snippets of the past twenty minutes floating in the back of my mind, but trying to pull them out felt like they were a thousand pounds.

"…work on it?" Jack whispered.

I hadn't realized that he was talking to

me until that moment. With my foggy brain, I couldn't even begin to bring together what he had been talking about. I just turned to him and said, "What?" Right after I said it, I noted that I was just a step away from yelling—in the middle of class.

"Tom! Jack!" the teacher yelled as I jumped out of my seat. He sighed. "Just get out of my class," he ordered, hands on his temples.

As we left the classroom, Jack rolled his eyes in my direction. "You got me kicked out of class, again," he complained. I didn't bother responding. I didn't have the energy, and he gets himself kicked out on a regular basis.

"You're the one always getting me kicked out of class," I mumbled, after a few silent moments.

He laughed and slapped me on the back. "I know," he said, grinning, "I just like to mess with you. You must be fucking tired, 'cause you totally believed me."

I rubbed my temples. I didn't even register anything that Jack had been saying. "What? Whatever," I replied. "I was up late working on… the project." That was almost the truth. I just wasn't up late last night.

"Oh, yes, the infamous project—the very same project that got us kicked out of class again," he pointed out.

"Wha…?" I contemplated out loud. Finally, the pieces began to put themselves together. Of course, I thought, he was talking about the project.

It didn't do me a lot of good to figure that out now; we were already outside of class and free to talk as we wished. It didn't matter that we were kicked out, anyway. Mr. Roth always forgot about the students he kicked out—namely Jack and I.

Jack gave me a quizzical look as my thoughts were slowly progressing.

I shook my head, trying to throw out the tiredness. "Sorry," I grumbled. "Still tired."

He replied, "Whatever, man. We gotta get down to business."

I raised an eyebrow. "Since when do you get down to business?"

"Hey," he countered, "if Hannah's involved, I'm down."

I laughed. He was never going to get over her. Although he could call her up, and she'd come flying out, he always wanted to do things the hard way, as if he didn't pine for her the way he did. I continued, "If you want to come over after school, we can look at it, just me and you. I don't want a repeat of yesterday…"

"Yeah, I thought Alicia was going to kill you," he skated over, as if it were old news.

I froze. "Wait, why?" I asked, desperately.

He shrugged, taken aback. "I dunno. I guess she just wanted you to be finished. I'm sure it's nothing. She does always have that scowl on her face…"

I glared at him angrily. He leaned back, pleased. "You're just jealous that she went out with me and not you," I countered. I know that he had noticed her beauty right with me. We had been in the same room. But he ignored me. Had he been onto something, it was hard to say how I felt about that. Even if could vocalize it, it definitely was not something that I would share with Jack.

Instead, we talked about his upcoming basketball tournament, my dad's pressure to go to Princeton or some Ivy-League school I'd suffocate in, the damn cold weather of Minnesota, and the hot-ass girls that would walk by. I was never all that into the latter—talking about it at least. That was probably because two-thirds of my friends were girls, and I was afraid of being slapped. I sure thought about it, though. It was nice sometimes to talk with Jack's pheromone-infested brain. Sometimes is a key word.

I could hardly believe that the bell rang when it did, for I had only felt minutes pass. Jack, however, instantly shot up, as if he had been watching the clock.

"I gotta meet Hannah, see ya!" he explained as he shuffled off. It never ceased to amaze me how hot and cold he and Hannah could be.

That left me alone in the hallway as the other students filed around me. My muscles still ached from last night's sleep, and it took at least sixty seconds for me to get moving in the general direction of my classroom. Walking in the hallway felt like trying to walk through a concert crowd. Every sound was amplified, and everyone was walking too close.

I arrived right as the bell rang and I took my seat. Everyone around me was chatting away, but I stayed far and distant, fading slowly into darkness.

I didn't wake up until the bell rang to signify the end of the period. For a moment, I couldn't even remember where I was. The wonderful, warm feeling of ignorance disappeared quickly as the students were rushing past. I groaned in defeat as I stood up and discreetly stretched. I couldn't believe I'd slept through an entire period.

"You fell asleep again," someone very familiar pointed out behind me. I felt my blood try to push its way back to my face, but I refused to let it.

I turned around mid-stretch to see Alicia. "You noticed?" I asked, leaning on a desk beside her, attempting to be flirty. It was a complete fail that I regretted instantly. It wasn't even flirty.

She chuckled for just a second, but it wasn't warm; it was ice cold. "Everyone noticed." She saw the panicked look on my face, and added, "Except for the teacher, of course." I almost saw traces of a real smile behind her eyes, but I must've imagined it. Her face betrayed no melancholy.

I breathed a sigh of relief. She continued, "You know, one of these days, I hope you get caught."

I attempted a little wit. "Yes, but if I did, I

wouldn't be free on Saturday nights." I winked at her. She didn't even notice. While I'd been trying to hint, she had grabbed paper from her bag and was scribbling on it. Next time, I swore I'd make sure she was paying attention.

"You aren't free Saturday nights, anyway," she stated, without looking up from the paper. "You're too busy working on 'the project.'" She stopped writing for just a moment to put air-quotes around "the project." She handed the paper to me. "Well, here's today's assignment. See you later." Then, she merely walked off.

I crumpled up the piece of paper in frustration. Stupid Jack, I thought. How come he gets all the fucking girls, and I can't even get the nerdy, Asian chick? Well, the hot, nerdy, Asian chick. I knew I shouldn't have thought of her like that; nobody seemed to be able to get her. I couldn't help it, though. Jack got every girl he winked at, and I couldn't get the one I wanted.

I picked up my bag and shuffled off to the next class. I put down my bag at my next desk and immediately placed my head on the cold faux-wood. I fully expected to fall asleep, and I did. The fact that I was awoken by the bell thirty seconds later didn't help my foggy brain.

The teacher instantly began class. I stared at him and tried to comprehend what he was saying, but it was impossible. Before long, it was work time, and I had no idea what we were doing. I scrawled the assignment into my notebook, but after cracking open the textbook, all of the words blurred together into one meaningless story about José and Sandy and their seashells and dollars and thirty miles past the ice cream prices. I looked at my notebook. There were only lines.

I continued to focus on the lines, trying to stay up, and drew more. Suddenly, the bell rang and I jumped. I couldn't even feel the time pass by.

I unknowingly ended up in my next classroom. The world continued to revolve around me while I sat in a wondrous, white stupor. When it came to lunch, I couldn't even tell what time it was. By the time I made it to the cafeteria, everyone had settled into their little cliques.

I sat down next to Jack and zoned out. He failed to notice. Alicia waved her hand in front of my face. "Hey, are you there?"

I slowly turned to her and simply said, "No."

She laughed sarcastically. "Seriously, you should go to the nurse," she advised.

"Yeah," Hannah piped in, "There's apparently a mono epidemic going through."

I fake-coughed. "You're right. I'm sick," I replied.

"Will you be serious?" Alicia said as she gave me a menacing look. It was almost as if she cared. I knew better. She probably wanted to make sure she didn't get it.

I threw my hands up. "Okay, okay," I grumbled, "Although I'm sure it's nothing…"

"Just go to the nurse," she pleaded.

"Fine," I agreed. I stood up and meandered

over towards the nurse's office.

I stepped through the door. The nurse looked at me. She looked pretty zoned out herself. She must have been dealing with the mono all morning. "Tom, honey, you look positively awful," she commented. I had only been in a few times; it was amazing that she knew my name.

"Thanks," I muttered, and sat in a chair, rubbing my eyes.

"Well, what's wrong?" she asked.

I shrugged my shoulders. "Just tired," I explained.

She thought for a moment. "It could be the mono going around," she thought aloud. How did everyone know about this mono and not me? "Well, let's take your temperature." She performed the usual routine for sick kids, and, to no surprise, there was nothing wrong.

"Hm," she said, "well, I can't send you back to class, though." I gave her a puzzled look, but before I could ask, she continued, "I guess I'll just send you home."

"What?" I inquired. "Why?"

"Just think of it as a favor," she answered. "Now, go, I need to take care of other kids."

I stood there in shock as she walked off. Eventually, I turned around and headed towards my car. No one stopped me; no one asked me where I was going. I started my car and no one jumped out.

Then, I finally deemed that it was safe to go.

The roads were empty, with everyone in school or at work and arrived at home. I shut off the engine and sat there. I wasn't very tired anymore, but I had a new free day. I stared at my house—nothing too special. It was pretty small: two bedrooms, a bathroom, and one other room that served as the living room, kitchen, and dining room—combined without walls. The paint on the outside chipped at the edges, and the lilac bushes at the ends of the house were out of control. But it was home, and I really didn't want to be anywhere else. I jumped out of the car and walked back to my room.

Then, I opened the file labeled, "Vampire Movie".

CHAPTER TWO

"Dude," Jack declared, "where were you for sixth period?"

"The nurse sent me home," I explained, shrugging my shoulders.

"Aw, man," he complained. "How come you got to go home? That nurse is a bitch. She wouldn't even send Alicia home, and she went in right before lunch."

"She looked fine to me," I pointed out.

"I dunno. She said she has a headache," he elaborated. "Will you let me in already? I'm freezing!" He stood outside my door, fidgeting. He didn't have a jacket, even though he knew it was supposed to get colder every hour.

I countered, "Hey, you're the one who started the accusations."

He growled and pushed me out of the way. I laughed. He scowled. "So," he inquired, "did you work on it for your free hours?"

"Of course," I affirmed. I had diligently worked on it from the minute I opened it to the moment I opened the door for Jack. "Actually, it looks done to me, but it also looked done to me last night..." I let my voice trail off.

We sat down at the computer again. It was like déjà vu. We were doing this only yesterday. This time, when we watched it, I knew that I had to have it. We were running out of time. Whether that was true, it felt like it. I felt my heart ticking in my chest, and not beating. It was like a countdown, but I didn't know what happened at the end.

"Hm, I guess the quality fixed the other stuff," he commented. I nodded without taking my eyes off the screen, scanning for flaws.

It finished. I still stared at the screen. I started tapping my fingers on the desk. Silence followed.

"So?" I broke.

He contemplated for a moment. "Yeah, I can't find anything," he commented.

"Are you sure?" I asked. '"Cause we can look at it again—"

Jack interrupted me, "Tom! It's fine."

"It has to be better than fine. It has—"

"That's not what I meant!" he exclaimed. "There isn't anything wrong."

We sat there in silence for a moment. My heart began to ram itself against my ribcage. "Do you know what this means?" I posed.

"We're finally done?" he hopefully suggested, his face lighting up.

"No!" I began. "This is the beginning! We're done with the movie, but we can move onto Phase Two!"

He thought for a moment. "YouTube?" he asked, confused.

I smacked the back of his head. He groaned in pain. I tried not to think of how he could easily beat me up. "Think bigger! We've been planning this since the beginning!" I reminded him.

"Oh, you mean the stupid news thing," he realized. He wouldn't meet my eyes, but mine were in the stars with triumph.

"It's not stupid!" I began to rant on about our wonderful plan, hands flailing excitedly with every word. Jack, however, stared at me in disbelief.

"Tom," he explained coolly, "this is never going to work."

I looked at him with an icy stare. "What are you talking about?" I inquired, not actually paying much attention.

"We came up with that idea years ago. We were kids, you gotta grow up a bit, man," he said.

"Are you fucking kidding me? You're just going to give up? What the hell, *man*?" I quipped. I added the extra emphasis on *man* just to show my frustration with him. I always hated that he said things like *man*; it reinforced everyone's idea about him. I never said anything, but I always thought I should've. He may have been a bit daft, but it wasn't from drugs.

"Hey, dude," he said, attempting to calm me down, "I'm not giving up. Maybe we should go in a different direction, though…"

I shot him a filthy look. "Well, how about we get Hannah and Alicia over here? We'll see what they think." That was the end of that argument. I called them over the second I said the last word.

Within about forty-five minutes, Alicia and Hannah were back in my room. Now that I had cooled off, I felt kind of like a jackass. I had called them over here only yesterday with the same prospects. This time, I could purely hope that they agreed with the perfection. It was the final test.

I was confident when I spoke. "Yes, I know I called you over here just yesterday, but this time...this time, we have it." I told them last the last three words slowly, with more force.

I sat in the chair, assured, but when my hand hit the mouse, I began to shake a bit. As great as I may have sounded, I didn't want a repeat of last night. I was humiliated and downtrodden. But I pushed onto the video, and braced for the criticism afterwards.

It never came.

I looked at them. They looked back. "And…?" I inquired.

Hannah made a face and said, "I got nothing."

I looked at Alicia. "Yes, yes, I'm the *critical* one," she said, annoyed, "but I failed to find anything wrong." She smiled. This time, it looked like a real smile. My heart skipped a beat.

"We're done," I stated. The air stopped

moving around us as I could feel the mutual agreement in the room.

Instead of high-fives and laughs today, it was a more serious, quieter victory. Nonetheless, we had business to take care of.

"So," I said in the most business-like way I could manage, "the problem is: what do we do with the video?"

There was a pause. I know Jack was bitter over our earlier spat, but Alicia and Hannah didn't know that there was another option. I carried on, "First, we could just put it on YouTube with millions of other videos, gain small face time, and never be taken seriously." I took my gaze to Jack, and he shot me my filthy look from earlier right back at me. "Or, we could stick to the original plan."

"Well," Alicia immediately responded, "it's kind of obvious."

"Thank you," Jack said, "I knew that you'd have some sense." He continued to throw looks at me that made my face grow hot.

Alicia gave him a very odd look. "Of course I mean that we send it in." Jack's mouth dropped open. Alicia pushed on, "I mean...this is what we've been working for, right?"

My face grew a bit redder, not from anger this time, but from Alicia. She actually believed in my idea.

Hannah simply nodded. I could definitely see that she had no opinion of her own here. She wanted her limelight—one way or the other, it didn't matter. She only agreed to the video because of me and Jack, and because she wanted to be noticed. I never saw where her attention-seeking complex came from. She was one of the most popular girls in school, and everyone's eyes were always on her.

"Well," Jack relented, "I can see that I'm outnumbered." He impossibly became even bitterer about the whole situation. "Hey, maybe it will work. But, if it doesn't, we're sending it to YouTube, right?" he suggested.

"Of course we will," Hannah excitedly put in.

The world spun around me with a big smile plastered on my face. Everything I'd worked towards for over a year was finally becoming a reality.

The other three started to converse among each other, and I spun to my computer. I grabbed my box of miscellaneous cords and commenced sorting a few out. I stood up and walked back to my dad's room and grabbed the old camera that had a computer cable, but still ran on the old tapes. Luckily, there was still a tape inside. I had no idea what was on that tape, but it didn't really matter. If it had been there, forgotten for so long, I was sure it wasn't important.

On my way back to my room, I passed Alicia, and she only said, "I have to go. Bye."

My hand waved goodbye to her lazily. I

opened my mouth to bid her farewell, but nothing came out. She simply walked past me, and I stood there awkwardly, watching her leave. I waited until the heat in my face subsided before I went back to my work station.

I arrived back at the desk, and Jack and Hannah were still talking—a lot closer than I had left them. "You guys," I told them, "don't do any of that in here. Take it outside." I meant it jokingly, but even I could hear the drop of acid in my voice. I supposed I was a bit jealous. Jack always got the hot girl, as dumb as he was. Although Hannah and I were good friends, that's really all we would be. And Jack, who played her and most of all the other girls in the school, would always get her back.

Jack shot daggers at me from his eyes. However, Hannah stood up. "Yeah, I have a thing to do." She showed Jack a mischievous smile. "Bye, hun." Then, she left, leaving him only a wink. "Bye, Tom," she said to me innocently.

The second the door shut, Jack attacked me. "Son of a bitch!" he screamed, and pinned me to the ground, giving a hard punch to my arm.

Despite the pain, I still held a triumphant smile. I replied, "What? No kanoodling in my room."

Jack pulled his arm back to throw another punch, obviously aiming for my face. I cringed and tried to block. Instead, he groaned. "Whatever," he said in a huff. "I'm out."

"Oh, come on," I pleaded. "It was just a

joke."

He just gave me a look that made me feel like if he could shoot lasers through his irises, he definitely would. I cringed again, and he slammed the door.

That, however, couldn't spoil my good mood. I sat down at my computer and began the transfer from digital to old tape. I sat there, fidgeting, while the multiple hour process began. Every sound seemed louder than normal as the silence became physical around me. I even heard the front door open and shut softly.

"Why'd Jack leave so mad?" my dad called out. He was one of the best used car salesmen in Minnesota, even at too good of a price. To top it off, not only did he sell actual working cars, but he sold the most. He had this amazing ability to read people. He always knew where the deal-breakers were just by listening to his customers 'nonverbal signals. Unfortunately, and also quite frequently fortunately, he also used that wonderful power on my friends and me. He opened the door of my room, but stayed at the door. He was probably afraid something would appear from the mess and devour him.

I shrugged. "I wouldn't let him make out in my room," I explained simply.

"Hannah?" he asked. I swear he knew everything.

"Yeah, how'd you know?" I inquired, trying to peer into his mind, like he could unbelievably peer into everyone else's. Although, he could've probably just assumed. I'd only had three girls in my room before, and Hannah was the most frequent. She was also the only one who'd been in there in the past four months or so, not counting Alicia. She'd never been here without the entire gang, anyway.

"It's that dreamy look he gets in his eyes," he explained. "It only happens when you've got Hannah over." I mentally stored away that I may have some of his skills. I never knew what it was about Jack I noticed differently when Hannah was around, but the eyes made perfect sense.

I rolled my eyes at him. "You don't have to analyze my friends all the time, dad," I told him. "It's not like you're trying to sell them a car." I wasn't sure why I said that. It kind of amused me when he did, but sometimes things just fell out of my mouth. It was actually very common for that to happen.

"Don't be too sure 'bout that," he replied. "Besides, if I recall correctly—which I do—you asked me how I knew."

I hated when he was right. That's why I sat in silence. He continued, "How was school?"

Shit, I thought. I had forgotten that I went home early. I, nevertheless, was not going to tell him about that. He definitely believed in a hard-work principle. "Boring," I replied as nonchalantly as I could. That was always my reply, as it were always true.

"Hang in there, buddy," he said and ruffled my hair as he left.

I kind of wished he would've stayed. This process was incredibly long, and, although I didn't need to sit here, I felt magnetically drawn to it. My eyes, like they were held by strings, drew their way to the screen that only changed minimally.

"So, what are you working on?" he asked, and I almost jumped out of my chair. I didn't expect him to return—at least not within thirty seconds with the sound of crunchy potato chips. "Sorry," he apologized, "didn't mean to scare ya." He patted my head again. He'd found a spot to stand behind me.

I reached over and silently grabbed a couple of chips. I didn't put them in my mouth yet; my dad knew distraction techniques. He merely looked at me, expecting a simple answer. I had to tell him eventually. I just didn't know how he would take it.

He continued to stare at me. *Aw, crap,* I thought. *I'm stalling, and he can see it.* I tried putting the chips in my mouth, hoping he'd drop it, but the scene didn't change, except for getting more awkwardly silent. That's when I made the (semi)conscious choice to tell him about the plan. "Alright, so, you know the video we've been working on? Yeah, so, I kinda edited it in order to make it look real, and now we're going to send it in to CNN, and hopefully they'll think it's real and we'll get famous when we tell them it's all a joke, 'cause then Jack and Hannah can get some acting jobs, I can get an editing job, and Alicia...well, I don't know what she wants," I said as quickly as I could, taking as little breaths as possible. I immediately grabbed more chips and shoved them in my mouth, hoping to get out of any more questions.

He raised an eyebrow at me. "That's what you've been working on?" It was obvious that he didn't believe me. He's going to tell me it's dumb, or it won't work, or something... I contemplated before he began again. "Alright, knock yourself out." He smiled and left to sit in his chair to watch television—a television I would soon be on, I was sure of it. It didn't matter what anyone else said. I knew it would work.

I knew my dad didn't believe it for a second, but he was incredibly supportive to the end. I knew other parents weren't the same way, and I thanked the world every day that I had the dad that I did. I was surprised last year when he revealed that it was one reason my mom left. "She had such low self-esteem," he told me. "When I told her that she could do it, it became a huge fight." I saw tears start in his eyes, but he would never dwell on the sad things. He continued, "She would tell me that I was a liar and would throw lampshades at me." He rubbed an invisible bump on the top of his head, and we both laughed, despite the sad topic. Now, we didn't talk about her at all.

I still thought about her, even though I was little when she left. I'd only seen her once since then, when I was nine, but I still couldn't be sure it was her. I was supposed to be sleeping, but I tiptoed outside to see my dad pleading with a young woman sitting in a beat-up car with the boxes of things that we packed for my mom. She didn't look at him, and she didn't see me. She stared straight ahead at the side of the house, growing a dim yellow from the rising sun.

It always stuck in my mind how that woman looked before she left. She had the same color hair as I did, but straight, long, and messy. Her clothes were tattered and her hands gripped the steering wheel tightly. She had huge bags underneath her dark green eyes that only looked straight ahead. They were empty.

Suddenly, I was very, very lonely.

CHAPTER THREE

The four of us—meaning I—figured out a schedule to watch CNN for our story. We needed to be sure that there was someone on the channel at all times. Hannah was rich, so she could carry around her little mini-television. Her parents gave it to her when she was thirteen so she wouldn't get bored in school. It was hard to imagine how a girl like her could stand to be around Jack and I all the time. It's not like we were poor or anything, but she always was over at my few-room, sparsely furnished trash-heap of a house when she could be comfortably sitting on a couch designed by Ed Hardy or whoever was in right now, watching a television that covered her entire wall—stationed on a channel I'd never heard of, while sipping imported wine from a glass that was valued more than my computer.

It didn't matter to her, though. While she may have been rich, gorgeous, and attention-seeking, she was surprisingly good at heart. She was honest, dependable, and funny. Regardless of her motives, we could definitely depend on her to be watching CNN during the school day. Even the teachers wouldn't care. I swore that they were paid off to never get her in trouble.

Then, it was my turn. I would quickly drive home, and sit in my room at watch TV. It wasn't really much different than a normal day. I just needed to watch TV instead of my computer screen. Jack had basketball practice after school, so he didn't have time to vegetate like I did. Well, at least not immediately after school. At about eight o'clock, he agreed to call me and start his shift. He only went from eight to ten-thirty, though. He didn't believe in the project, anyway, so it wasn't a big loss.

After that, Alicia would start her schedule. She would watch from ten-thirty to four. She was on some weird polyphasic sleep schedule. It was cool and all; we had someone to watch while most of us slept. However, someone was going to have to wake up at four-in-the-fucking-morning to watch for a mere hour. Everyone thought that, since it was my brilliant idea, I should be the one to do it. Considering that no one else would volunteer, I knew that I had to surrender. Jack would pick up at five, listening while he jogged, and watching while he ate, but that one hour was definitely going to throw me off.

At any rate, we started the next morning. Of course, the first morning, despite the schedule, I watched CNN with hungry, hopeful eyes. I continued to watch even through Jack's shift. But after watching boring, meaningless stories about some country I didn't care about, some fire thousands of miles from my own city, and some child I would never meet, my eyes began to gloss over and I thought rationally. I sent it in last night, I figured. It actually has to take time to get there. Their mail probably hasn't even come yet. Not only that, but they need to sort through all of the other hopefuls, and weed out all of the fakes...except ours.

So, grudgingly, I got into my car and began the trek to school. I turned the radio up loud to the local top-40 station. Of course, it was some pop song about partying and getting drunk, but it definitely had an infectious rhythm. I drove a bit slower, considering how early I left. It made the trip to school just a little bit better. For once, I wasn't tired or grumpy when I returned to the jail of a high school, even though I had woken up two hours earlier than normal.

I still arrived a half hour early for school with nothing to do. I supposed I could've done my homework, but I hadn't done it my entire high school career, and I felt no pull to start doing it now—especially since I was on the brink of infamy. I settled for sitting near my first class on the floor, to people watch.

I saw a group of stereotypical freshman girls pass by. They were the popular ones, in short shorts and pink, even in the moderately cold weather. They talked exactly how you'd expect them to: "...and then Tami broke up with Eric because Shelly said she saw him making out with

Lana at Greg's party..." When they passed by my area, they gave me a look. It was almost as if I were a big spider they had to walk around.

I tried to channel my dad's skills. Their eyes on my clothes showed their apparent lack of responsibility from their parents. Their hands always gravitating toward their pocketed iPhones confirmed it. If I had to guess a car, I'd definitely pick something expensive and new. They would obviously get into something way over their heads, and wouldn't even graze on the consequences. Plus, their parents would probably bail them out, no matter what the monetary or personal cost.

I felt satisfied with my reading, but I knew my dad wouldn't be satisfied with it. He may have had a bigger heart than me. He would, without a doubt, work with them and actually trick them into something they could afford. I sighed and accepted that I would never be the same salesman as my father. Not that I wanted to be, anyway. I was never good at sales.

Eventually, the bell rang, and class started. When I sat in my seat, I was incredibly fidgety. It was like there was an itch under my skin, but something I didn't have an urge to take my nails to. It was surprisingly good feeling. I just knew that something was coming. My mind and my body had completely convinced itself that this was going to work. I could even justify it.

One, vampire fanaticism was at an all-time

high. This is what everyone wanted to believe. Two, life had begun to get boring, and everyone was looking for something to spice it up. Three, we did a pretty damn good job. That third one might have taken a bit of prideful liberty, but I truly believed it. It made spiders crawl beneath the deepest layers of my skin, as if it really happened to me.

I couldn't concentrate in class. It wasn't like yesterday when I was falling asleep every ten minutes. I just kept staring at the clock, out in the hall, at my phone, and anywhere else. I just expected something to explode at any second. Like there was supposed to be some kind of party to celebrate my—our—triumph.

But the bell rang, and nothing happened. I didn't lose hope. I continued on to my next class. And then my next class. Then my next. I was beginning to wind down.

Calm down, Tom, I told myself. *Again, their mail probably hasn't come yet. Besides, they probably have tons of videos to get through each day.* No matter what I told myself, I still couldn't stop the sinking fear that maybe we weren't good enough. The elation I'd felt before deflated itself until I was on the ground. It was almost as if the world needed to compensate itself for my feeling of happiness by replacing it with just as much depression. It stayed with me until I arrived home to start my shift.

I sat in front of the television with a bag of

nacho chips and a chill down my spine. I heaved out a big sigh before I turned on the television, but somehow I knew it wouldn't work. I imagined how the newscast would've gone. They would've probably stopped all stories to run ours. They'd most likely even get to it during my shift—which was how it should've been. I sat and watched. I kept watching. I even held my bladder, in order to catch every moment of it. Even through my own disbelief, I kept watching, clinging onto to smallest thread that I might be wrong. Please, please let me be wrong, I pleaded to no one in particular.

Then, Jack called. He was ready to take his shift. "Alright," I responded and disconnected the call. However, I kept watching. There was invisible superglue, sticking me to that very spot, in front of the television, with its hooks embedded into my eyes. I watched it continuously, only stopping once when my bladder couldn't take any more abuse. Even after that, I raced back to my spot and continued to watch until all of the words blurred together into a buzz and the visual feed turned white in my mind.

I awoke to the sound of my phone ringing. I instantly bolted upright and turned the television on, knowing it was time. I saw nothing. I took out my still ringing phone and saw that it was just my alarm. It was four o'clock in the goddamn morning, and we still had nothing. I looked at the TV that my dad must have turned off. I stared at it, not absorbing any of it. Everything was still normal. I cursed quietly.

I quickly ran to the bathroom, did my business, and returned. Still, nothing had changed. I began to pull my hair out from frustration. I worked hard. This wasn't how it was supposed to happen. Regardless, my eyes stayed glued to the screen until about six-fifteen. Then, I gave up and readied myself for a disappointing day at school.

Nothing could capture my interest. I knew that it was over, finitely. I just went through school as I had two days ago, like a zombie. I could barely remember moving from one class to another. The only recognition I had was when Alicia complained about all of the things she could've been doing instead. Then, I began to feel like shit. I dragged all of my friends down with me in this little pointless quest. Jack had been right; it was never going to work.

I still turned on the television when I got home, but I had most of my focus on other things. I made a proper dinner, I browsed the internet, and threw things around in my room, not actually cleaning anything, but made more space. I still kept an ear open, though—just in case. Eventually, before bed, I gravitated toward my computer and opened up the sacred file.

I watched it twice or three times, I didn't quite remember. I kept my eyes glued to the screen as I had to the TV. Every ounce of my conscious effort had gone into this movie, whether I'd worked on it or not. My mind was always on this or on the aftermath. The awards, the recognition, the job offer. I wouldn't need to go to school. I wouldn't need to search for a job. Everyone would know my name, and those freshman girls wouldn't look at me like I was a leper. Although I wanted nothing to do with them, the look was enough to make me despise them. And, given the chance, trick them into buying a car they couldn't afford.

After it, I collapsed into bed, fading into a dream as black as my mood.

When my alarm went off at four, I ignored it and didn't get up until I had to get ready for school. I still checked CNN for a moment, but I knew that it wasn't happening. It was over.

It seemed that everyone else lost interest, as well. Hannah didn't even bring her television to school, and I didn't call her out on it. Alicia didn't complain about what else she could've been doing—probably because she had been doing it. Jack didn't make a reference to it whatsoever. At least they had the decency not to bring up the dreaded Plan B...yet. I could see it in Jack's eyes, but I noticed how he almost always whispered to Hannah before saying something to me.

I got through the school day, but it couldn't have ended soon enough. I just wanted to sit at home and lounge. I deserved it. I did all that work and had nothing to show for it. When I arrived home, I surprised myself by tuning the TV to CNN. I couldn't even believe that I was watching it. At that point, I hated the pompous little reporter talking about whatever election no one cared about. I had to hold myself from bellowing out at him, even if he couldn't have heard me.

CHAPTER FOUR

I loved my friends, few as they were. They were loyal, decent people. I didn't use them, but there were a couple perks to being best friends with Jack and Hannah. They were popular and hot as hell. That also meant that I could go to the best parties. I wasn't hated or anything, but I had a few connections in the crowd. However, without them, I never would've been invited to Carter's party. Honestly, I couldn't pick Carter out in a crowd. I'm not sure I ever met him, but I knew he threw the best parties.

I drove to the house silently, by myself. I preferred it that way. I always wanted Jack to find his own way home. If I drove there, it was understood that I would drive back. When I got there, I took the house and sized it up. It stood alone, so I never got lost on my way there. In nice, little suburbia, it was a sign of definite money to be left without neighbors. It had a gigantic driveway with an endless forest behind it. The house itself was large. It was two floors, plus a basement. It had at least eight bedrooms, four bathrooms, and twelve other rooms I'd never heard of. It was all white and tastefully lit. The whole area was covered with a perfect green lawn—which didn't make a lot of sense to the lower-middle class me. However, whenever the snow was gone, even for a minute, the gardeners were out and the green was unnaturally—well, green. Well, I'm sure it was perfect before the crazy young adults tore it up with their car tires.

It was the perfect place for unsupervised teenage parties. That would probably be the reason that they happened so damn often.

Jack had told me that I needed to go to the party. I was still a little down about the video flop. Maybe he was right; it might have been time for me to loosen up. It had been a whole week. That's why I found myself driving up the infinite driveway—tasting the ear-splitting music, the drunk vomiting, and the wonderful, meaningless sex in the upstairs bedrooms in the air from my slightly cracked window.

I loved going to the parties. Although I wasn't exactly in a partying mood that day, I came. I normally stood in the dark corners and watched everyone make a complete fool of their self. Sometimes, I would even laugh or make a witty comment. The most enjoyable part, however, was definitely the atmosphere. I know my body wanted to be right there on the floor, grinding on some girl with a beer in my hand and a ridiculous hat on my head, but my mind knew better. Just being there was enough. My cold corpse came alive on nights like these. Even if I never took a step from the wall, a couple beers and the ability to see the perfect people at the worst satisfied my deepest hunger.

I parked my car somewhere close, but definitely far enough away from the other cars. I definitely couldn't handle my car being destroyed by some drunken teenager. Besides that, I know my car would look infinitely worse in comparison to the other cars.

I opened my glove box and moved around the few papers until I found the cigarette in the back. I wasn't addicted. I'd never even had a pack myself, but I always found someone to give me one to stow away for nights like these. I lit it and took a puff. It was still disgusting in taste, but I knew it would be worth it in thirty seconds. I took a swig of water to wash down the ashy taste and took another drag. Soon enough, the world slightly tilted itself to the left and the right. It wasn't enough to make my head hurt or even hinder me in any way, but it was almost a precursor of the upcoming alcohol about to enter my veins.

I finished my cigarette and threw it onto the lawn amongst the already growing pile of trash. It was amazing how far a mess could spread. I locked the doors and trudged up the lawn. A girl —nice legs and a dress that was, without a doubt, about to be ruined—ran past me. I wasn't sure her motives, but I definitely enjoyed the view for a few seconds. Those gorgeous legs ran with such grace, even with those absurd heels, that I began to think,

Maybe this won't be so bad.

The door was wide open. Even though it was cold out, the scarcely furnished room was radiating heat and sweat. I was pretty sure that the air was forty-five percent alcohol, fifteen percent rap, ten percent hormones, and the rest was breathable oxygen. I could feel the corners of my mouth turn up slightly. This was a place I wanted to be. This was a place I was born to be.

"Yo," called a buzzed Jack, "Tom-man made it!" For some reason, he always changed his nickname for me with his different stages of intoxication. He was level one for now. I'd begun a system for Jack. I had it down to a tee. It never failed. If he talked to me for ten seconds, I could tell you exactly how many drinks he'd had within one or two. Although, you could normally find out just by looking at the time. His drinking was like clockwork.

I searched around until I found him. Unsurprisingly, he had his arm around Hannah. She had a huge, silly grin on her face. She never minded being Jack's arm candy. I decided to be a little reckless. "So, you guys back together already?" I asked, sly grin on my face. I knew I was skating on thin ice, even with a level one Jack. If the answer wasn't favorable, I could see a black eye in my future.

Jack bellowed out a deep laugh. "I don't know. Baby...?" He leaned down to Hannah's face. I heaved a sigh of relief. It almost felt like I'd already had a drink or two. Well, with the alcohol I was no doubt breathing in, I might've had the equivalent.

She pushed him away, still smiling. "Not even, Jack," she corrected. Jack just shrugged and took another gulp of what I assumed was beer. We stood there awkwardly for a three seconds. Before another second passed, he was beckoned by some of his other jock friends. Being normal Jack, he just left Hannah. She didn't seem to mind. I watched her in awkward silence. She wasn't drunk or flirty or anything you would expect her to be at a party —except happy. I tried to channel my dad amidst the thick air and loud bass. I don't think she had any alcohol at all. It did seem a bit out of character. She never got drunk at parties, but she has been known to take a shot or two.

"Tom," she said loudly. I snapped out of my analytical state.

"Sorry, what?" I replied as my face went red.

Just then, Jack called out, "Tommy, come take a shot with us!" He always tried to get me in with his buddies at level two. He must've had a few more drinks right before I arrived, and they were just taking hold.

I didn't mind, though. They never stopped me. They let me come, anyway. I walked over to the group of six or so jocks. One with black hair poured me a shot, a bit lacking. "A baby shot for little Tommy," he said, and they all laughed, including Jack. I laughed a bit, too. It was all in good fun. Besides, I didn't mind a smaller shot. This particular area smelled very much like Jose Cuervo, and I knew Jose very well.

We clinked the shot glasses together and downed them. I realized as it touched my lips, that I had no chaser. Good going, Tom, I told myself. Well, here goes nothing. The burning hit my tongue and ran down my throat. I instinctively wanted to gag, but held it in for appearance. I apparently did a very bad job because Jack laughed and handed me his beer. I took a quick swig and let the lukewarm brew wash down the taste of smoke and vomit.

I shook my head and let the warm feeling pulsate in my chest. Immediately, they held the glass out to me again, and the black-haired jock asked, "Another?"

"Later," I replied and instantly walked away before I could hear any taunts designed to change my mind.

I found my way back to Hannah who had only moved a few feet to stand against a wall—my old standby. I took a spot next to her and we sat in relative silence, just watching the crowd. I had a hard time focusing on any one thing, letting the little alcohol take a small bit of my consciousness away. It wasn't enough to do any real harm, but it was enough to make me feel happy.

It was also enough for me to miss what Hannah said to me. It was like a faint buzzing coming from her vocal cords. I turned to her and said, "I'm sorry?"

She laughed and grabbed my arm. Her skin was very soft and surprisingly warm. She weaved me in and out of the drunkards, breaking through couples and spilling bit of drinks that nobody seemed to notice—probably because they were spilling enough themselves.

She eventually was able to toward the wide open glass patio door. It was covered in food and fingerprints, and, with a party like this, I was surprised it was still intact. The second the cool air hit my skin, my pores heaved a heavy breath of relief. I hadn't realized how hot it had gotten in there, but the frigid oxygen now piercing my skin felt like a welcoming blanket, with the opposite effect.

There were, of course, quite a few rowdy people outside as well. The noise wasn't nearly as concentrated out here, but I could still hear almost the same noises. It was definitely quiet enough for Hannah and me to have a proper conversation, but we just stared at the half- and fully- naked bodies splashing drunkenly in the pool. It was amazing that they could stand to be in that water which was undoubtedly colder than the air itself. I wasn't even sure that the pool was supposed to be set up this time of year, but I suppose with so much money, you learn to stop caring.

It was almost funny. I knew it was bad; I was watching people have sex—which quite a few of them were, discretely as they may or may not have been trying. I don't know how many patrons also noticed, but the consensus was apathy. Everyone seemed to let their inhibitions go.

Hannah let out a sigh. "Teenagers."

"Would it be a stretch to argue that you are one?" I asked, chuckling.

She punched me in the arm. It was a lot different than when Jack punched me. He left bruises.

"Yes," she replied, faking annoyance, "but I never act like that." She gestured toward the pool, and I looked away quickly, like I could erase my own indecent watching by acting fast enough.

"True," I agreed. "You just like to dance on tables and grind on other random teenagers." None of that was true, of course, but I was having fun.

"Oh, and snort lines of coke with a beer bong taped to my mouth," she continued.

"Don't forget to put the lampshade on your head."

"That was one time!" she exclaimed, smiling.

"That you remember," I said with a devilish grin.

She punched me again. I punched her back, much lighter than I would to Jack—or even Alicia, for that matter. Not that it seemed like I'd ever get to touch her in any capacity. But Hannah seemed so much more fragile. She was very thin; she wasn't runway model skinny, but more like a regal thin, like she belonged on a pedestal.

We both laughed until it just died off. We sat in more silence for a few moments. "So, why'd you assume that me and Jack were back together?" she asked.

She caught me a little off-guard. I didn't have an answer for her right away. She was staring at me, so I cleared my throat. "I dunno..." I said, trying to be truthful. "I guess I just kinda asked. I didn't mean anything by it. I just wanted to poke fun at Jack a little more. You guys are always together."

She laughed again. "Great best friend," she responded.

"Hey! I'm a good friend!" I defended. "We hang and talk about girls and shit. And I get drunk with him at parties where I have no friends!"

"I wouldn't call taking one shot getting drunk," she pointed out. "Especially a baby shot."

My face grew hot. I didn't know she could hear that. I wondered who else heard. Not that it mattered that much—I already knew that the two people here that mattered had heard.

She continued to laugh. I watched her laugh. She wasn't doing her normal giggles. It was like there was a legitimately funny secret—a wonderful, pensive secret. I rarely got to see this part of her. She was always the fun-loving, rich, pretty girl. She was especially pretty when she laughed like that. I watched her lips move as she let out the laughter and had the urge to kiss her.

I instantly shook the thought away, attributing it to the alcohol. She was one of my best friends, and Jack's girlfriend. Besides, my mind was set on Alicia for some reason. I guess my slightly intoxicated mind found the similarities between the two girls: same height, same length of straight, soft hair, same soft, stroke-able cheeks, and the same full lips.

I quickly tried to keep my mouth moving to avoid any more troubling thoughts. "Anyway, guys are allowed to be mean to each other," I explained. "It's what we do."

"Of course."

Someone then ripped between us and puked off the balcony, then rushed back into the party the second he finished. It was my turn to laugh. "I'm thinking that maybe I won't drink any more tonight."

"Good plan," she concurred.

There was always a silence that hung between us that I longed to fill. Our conversations were repeatedly short, regardless of how much I enjoyed talking with her.

I opened my mouth to speak and even surprised myself with the words that came out. "He loves you, you know." I regretted it immediately and looked away. She didn't respond right away, and only took long, slow breaths. Despite the noise of the party, I could still hear the displacement of the air she took in. Eventually, I deemed it safe to look at her. Her gaze was locked far away into the stars.

She didn't look at me when she replied. "I know."

As if on cue, Jack stumbled outside. "Yo, Tom-Tom," he said, putting his arm around Hannah's waist, "you getting 'cozy with mah girrrl?" He was definitely at level four, and, with the bottle of beer in his hand, his must be rapidly approaching level five. Hannah just rolled her eyes and made a drinking gesture at me. I chuckled. He didn't even notice. He took another swig of beer— spilling a bit down his shirt.

"Oh, definitely," I lied. Or am I really lying to myself? I asked, but I tried to pretend that I never needed to think that. There wasn't much he would do, anyway. Plus, he'd be getting cozy with some other slut before level six, and he was definitely getting past level six tonight. It was barely past eleven, and Jack would never stop partying until he crashes at two. At the start of our partying, I used to worry about him. At some point, though, he needed to take care of himself.

Jack pulled on Hannah. "Come on, babeeeee," he told her, "I gotta show you some peepsss…" I don't think either of us really had any idea what he was talking about, but she didn't struggle too much. She waved at me and headed back inside beside Jack.

I felt very lonely right then. Although there were people ten feet away down in the pool and people three feet away on the other side of the window, it felt more like they were on a television screen. It was like I was watching a movie by myself. I did that all the time, being the movie buff I was, but it was always nicer to do it with someone else. Although, they always got angry with my amount of talking.

I longed for another drink—or six, but I knew I wasn't going to be drinking tonight. The putrid smell of vomit wafting from the ground certainly made sure of that. I at least wanted a cigarette. The thought took me aback a bit. I never needed nicotine to calm down or slow my breathing. But tonight was different, even if I couldn't pinpoint why. Unfortunately, I had to settle for watching the people in and around the pool.

I couldn't stand to look that way for too long and tore my eyes away from the frisky couples. I turned the other direction, to the house. I could see people pressed up against the windows, either with other hands racing across their backs, or just slumping over, done for the night. I just stared inside the house, as if I could pierce into the fray with my gaze. One girl saw me looking and gave me a little wave. She must've thought I was staring at her. I quickly felt embarrassed and tried to look away. When I looked back, she was still looking at me. She didn't look disgusted or annoyed. She just looked pretty. She strode out of the view of the window and what looked like the direction of the back door. Quickly, I straightened up my clothes, secretly hoping she'd keep me company.

I saw a high-heeled shoe poke out of the doorway, followed by the girl. I watched her approach me. She walked terribly well, leading me to believe she hadn't had any drinks yet.

"Hey, I'm Lisssa," she introduced. She was a very well-behaved drunk. However, that extra s's clued me in. It sounded like a snake.

"Tom," I replied. She smiled a very large smile at me. She wore a very fitting dress, red, but not any expensive material. It was kind of a breath of fresh air.

"You're cute," she said, still smiling. It was a cute smile, but it was almost kind of creepy. It was like she wanted to eat me up.

But the comment surprised me. I didn't think I was ugly, by any means, but it definitely wasn't a comment I was used to. "Thanks," I said quietly.

She looked around a bit—almost as if she were about to make a drug deal. "So," she finally said, "I heard that this guy's parent's bed is uber-comfy. Wanna check it out?"

She was so forward. It was kind of shocking. Lisa was full of surprises. My body definitely was telling me, yes. It had been a long while, even if my life for the past year or so revolved around the fake taping of a porno video. When I opened my mouth, my body and my mind didn't seem to agree. "I don't want to have sex with you." Did I really say that? And did I really say it like that? The worst part was that I meant it.

She didn't seem fazed. She shrugged, and quickly moved onto another boy that was taking a break outside. I stood there, alone and speechless. I couldn't believe it. She was a grade-A slut. I'm surprised Jack hadn't gotten to that yet. Or, maybe he had.

My thoughts didn't dwell on her for long. My mind drew itself toward other girls, mostly Alicia and a bit of Hannah. I couldn't comprehend why or what it was, but I could only guess that Alicia wouldn't go for a player. She hadn't fallen for Jack, after all. With Hannah, I actually cared what she thought of me. She always told me about how she loved the contrast between Jack and me, and she could always get a good break from either of us by talking to the other. I knew that hooking up with Lisa would just be step one to becoming Jack.

I stood there for a good minute or so before I jumped from a loud crash. One second later, there was an entire lamp in front of me. All I could hear was laughter. I believe that my own was there as well. I looked inside, and almost everyone had stopped what they were doing to laugh at the situation. It wasn't their house, so why should they care?

That's when I decided that it was about time to head home. I checked my watch; I'd been there for about two hours. However, it was good enough. I looked to the side of the house. I could have easily gone around, but I groaned and felt compelled to say good-bye. I stepped through the doorway and it felt like I was walking through gelatin. The air was thick and smelled worse than the decaying vomit outside. Luckily, I found Jack and Hannah within minutes.

Hannah clung to Jack like girlfriends do, but I could see that she may have been supporting him a bit.

"Tttttttommm…" Jack moaned. He was getting to level seven by now. He was going to drink himself into a coma one of these days. He had a huge smile on his face, and I decided to leave him be for the day—not that any lecturing would get through.

I ignored Jack for the time being, and said to Hannah, "Well, I suppose you didn't need the rest of the lamp, anyway…" I laughed.

As she giggled back at me, I already missed the laugh I'd heard on the patio. "Right! I've got the shade, what's the point of the stupid thing?" We laughed.

Jack mumbled something very excitedly, but I had no idea if he was using real words. "Of course, honey," Hannah said. I looked at her to clear up the confusion, but she shook her head and mouthed, I don't know.

"Yeah," I said, knowing he wouldn't remember it in five minutes. "I'm leaving."

"Mmmmm…" was his response.

Hannah let go of Jack and took about a minute to make sure he could stand on his own for a short time. He swayed, but stayed where he was. "Night," she said and gave me a big hug. It was a bit awkward at first. I didn't hug much. But, in the end, I let myself hold my arms around her for a second. It was a bit nice that she smelled like lilacs and not like beer and sweat.

"Bye," I replied and left.

CHAPTER FIVE

Life went on as normal. I'd finally come down from my high and up from my low about the video. I was surprised at how similar everything seemed, even though my time wasn't taken up by the video. I still thought about it a lot, but it didn't excite me as it did once.

All the extra time I had now seemed to fill up with meaningless tasks. I spent time watching television, as a normal teenager should. I took the effort to clean up my room. I spent hours on Facebook. I no longer went to school in a tired stupor. And, yet, none of my homework was done.

Jack kept pestering me to post the video to YouTube. I continuously told him I'd get to it, which I would. I really needed some relaxing time, and some time to calculate how I could still make it work.

I was sitting in math class scribbling nothing on the margins of my homework. I got to about the third question and got bored. Suddenly, I noticed someone was standing in front of me. I looked up and it was Mr. Nelson.

He stared at me, his irises lasers, burning my skin. He didn't say anything, but beckoned me to follow. Mr. Nelson was nice, but a little creepy. He had mostly black hair, with a little grey, and it was starting to bald out. He was tall and a bit pudgy, and he had a beard. I always saw his eyes following the girls, and I swore he was looking down their shirts.

He took me out into the hallway. "Tom," he said, like every other teacher. It always made my skin burn, and although I didn't believe in homework, it always made me feel like I did something wrong. "You've got a D in my class. You've almost got an F, but considering you get an A on every test, you're skating by."

That did make me feel a little cool. I almost wished he'd say that in front of the whole class, just so they could know how much smarter I am. I didn't speak my mind, however, for fear of getting in more trouble. I only shrugged.

"Do you even care? I can work with you, get your grades up," he replied. I couldn't be sure of his motives. I wasn't a hot, young girl, so I wasn't too positive that he wanted to do it for my benefit. But I could see how my bad grades could make him look bad. I didn't really care, though. I had no interest in pursuing a career with math, and, as far as I was concerned, I did not believe in the school system.

Of course, I went by my old standby answer to get the teachers off my back, and have them feeling good. "Yeah, I know," I said, the reply automatic. "I've been going through some stuff lately. I don't really want to talk about it,"—I learned to add that last part two years ago when my English teacher tried to talk out my feelings with me—"but if you give me a few days to catch up, I'm sure I can."

He nodded, satisfied. As with most teachers, he'd learn that I'd never even attempt to put it together. I had more important, creative things to keep my attention. He wouldn't bother me again.

When I got home, I sat down at my computer and decided it was time to let the news thing go, and start in on the YouTube project. I was editing a teaser trailer for the release of our video when my phone buzzed in my pocket. I waited to see if it would continue buzzing for a call. I was surprised when it did. Nobody called anymore; it was all texting.

I pulled it out and looked to see who it was. It was a private name and a number I didn't recognize. I started to put it away, but I was incredibly bored. I decided to just answer it, knowing that it was going to be a solicitor of some sort.

"Hello?" I told the receiver in a cold, bored voice.

"Is this Tom?" said an adult, female voice.

"Yeah, who's this?" I questioned.

"This is Linda, from the CNN stories department," she replied. I stopped in my tracks, and revamped my attitude. She continued, "I'm calling to schedule a meeting about the videotape you sent in." I opened my mouth, but couldn't find a response. "Tom? Are you still there?"

"Yes!" I shouted quickly. I began to sweat.

"Looking through the schedule, I believe that we have Tuesday open at the local office in Minneapolis. Is that okay for you?" she said and waited for a response.

She didn't have to wait long. "Yes, that's fine, what time?" I responded quickly.

"Eight-AM?"

"That's great," I said, still in a hurried panic.

"Alright, I'll see you then. Thanks, Tom." She hung up.

I continued to stand as a statue. I didn't remember to hang up the phone until I heard the busy tone. The second I put the phone down, I picked it back up again. I pushed the first speed dial.

"Hell—"

I never gave him the option to finish his greeting. "Jack! You'll never guess what happened!" I exclaimed into the phone.

"You got laid," he answered, bored.

"Bastard," I insulted, but continued eagerly. "No..." I proceeded to fill him in on the phone conversation with Linda. He didn't say anything for a while.

"You mean...it worked?" he managed to choke out in disbelief.

I had a huge smile on my face, and although

he couldn't see it, I was sure he could hear it. "Of course it did!" I replied. He didn't say anything for a while. I knew it would work, I thought. I should've never lost faith.

"You are aware that today is Sunday right?" he asked. I thought for a moment. I confirmed it. He continued, "Which means, you only have two days."

"So?" I asked, too wrapped up in my own fantasy.

"You have two days to get ready," he explained.

"You mean, 'we,' right?"

"No, I don't mean 'we.'" he responded. "I'm supposed to be dead, remember?" I could hear just a hint of bitter pride in his voice. You know, I wanted to say, I didn't make this movie alone… However, I bit my tongue and let him continue. "And, Hannah is a vampire, so you can't have her either." I heard him stifle a chuckle.

I gritted my teeth. "Will you at least drive to the city with me?"

He laughed. "Sure, buddy. I'll talk to you later." He hung up, still laughing,

I slammed the phone down, angrily. I started grumbling. There was one more person. I flipped open my phone and scrolled down two names. I hesitated on the send button. My thumb twitched and I hurriedly put the ringing phone to my ear.

"Hello?" Alicia answered. She almost

sounded normal.

"Hey, it's Tom," I replied.

"Yeah, I know." She wasn't normal. I guess I imagined it. It was like she had the world on a string. "What's going on?" she asked when I didn't say anything.

"Oh! Right!" I had forgotten to tell her about the call. I filled her in on the situation. "So, can you come?" I asked.

"Let me see..." I heard some wicked fast typing in the background. "Nope, can't. Sorry," she replied quickly, as if she weren't actually sorry.

"Are you kidding?" I complained. "What do you have going on?"

"Well, besides *school*—you know, that thing we go to Monday through Friday—I have my private flute lessons," she said matter-of-factly. I flushed and thanked the heavens that we were on the phone.

"Oh, come on," I protested, knowing it was useless. "Everyone knows that you're probably already the world's best flute player."

"And I didn't get that way by slacking off," she said, sounding almost angry. "But, on the bright side, it's supposed to be forty-eight degrees that day."

"Well, that's a good break. We haven't broken into the forties all month," I commented.

"I've noticed."

After that, I'd pretty much exhausted all conversation topics. We sat in awkward almost-silence before we decided to disconnect the call. I had a big smile on my face. That was two successful calls in one night. I sat in unconscious bliss for about thirty seconds before I jumped up in a panic. I didn't know how I was going to pull this off. I didn't know what kind of clothes I should wear, how early I should arrive... Then, a school bus of a thought hit me. I had school on Tuesday, like I did almost every other Tuesday.

My mouth began to shoot out numerous profanities when I heard the front door unlocking. My dad stepped in. That was exactly the thing I was dreading. I didn't mind missing school, but my father sure hated it. Crap, crap. I panicked. It was now or never. I ran up to him and explained the whole situation in one breath. Panting, I stared at him, waiting for an answer.

"So, wait, is this some kind of job interview, or...?" he asked.

"Kind of..." I replied without meeting his eyes. My socks became very interesting right then.

"And you're going to miss school?" he clarified.

"Yes." I stared at him now. It wasn't a hard challenge-me-if-you-dare look or an I'll-go-even-if-you-say-no look; I wasn't like that. It was more of a you've-always-been-supportive-why-stop-now stare.

He sighed. I smiled. It was the exact sigh I was looking for. "Fine," he replied, "but, you have to get your homework in advance." I groaned. He raised an eyebrow.

"Okay!" I raised my arms in surrender. I quickly retreated to my room before he could change his mind. I knew I wouldn't do my homework, anyway. I began to rummage through my small pile of clothes I left on the floor of my closet. Anything that looked somewhat dressy, I threw onto the bed. I turned around to face the small mound on my bed. It was hopeless. I've never been good with fashion—or business for that matter.

"Sh—" My dad stepped into my room. I let the word trail off. He looked at me, then at the pile of clothes on the bed.

"Need some help?" he asked.

"Yes," I said simply. He began to explain about looking good and trying to sell. At first, I rolled my eyes, but he explained that I was trying to sell something: my story. He then explained wrinkles and how absolutely horrifying they were. Oddly enough, I listened to him. I saw his eyes light up. He was actually enjoying himself. Maybe he was happy that I was interested in learning something about what he does, even if it was clothes. In the end, I had a dark red button up shirt, black pants, and a black tie.

"Thanks, Dad," I said awkwardly without looking at him. I'm a guy. We aren't good at this sort of thing.

He ruffled my hair. "No prob."

I rolled my eyes again. He may be a business

man, but deep down, he was a father, and that meant that he had to try to be cool. He left with a big smile on his face.

I stared at the clothes and decided that there was nothing else I could really do. I followed him to the living room. I wanted him to have this father-son moment to last as long as it could. If everything went according to plan, we wouldn't be having a lot of these.

He was, of course, watching television, with potato chips and a soda. I collapsed next to him. We watched some history something-something. It didn't actually look that bad. It was about Ancient Egypt.

"So," he finally said, "what made you finally decide that you like to hang with your old man?" I had to struggle to not roll my eyes. He put emphasis on hang to let me know that he was using the correct terminology.

"Well…" I thought for a moment before I continued. I could come clean right away. Let him know that we probably won't be spending much more time together, but then he might not think it's not sincere. What else could I tell him? I could lie and say that I just realized what a wonderful, cool dad he is, and I'm sorry I never paid him much attention. Well, that's not a total lie. He is a wonderful, cool dad…

I shrugged my shoulders. It was noncommittal, and I didn't have to lie or make him feel bad. He laughed.

"You're a cool dad," I said, and know that made him smile, even if I didn't see it.

The night went by quickly, a bit too quickly. The next day was a blur, as well. Every hour was an excited, shaking second. It was just like when I first sent the video, only I had I sure answer, and that made all of the difference.

When it got to Monday night, I had everything ready to go. My clothes were hung up and ironed. I had another copy of my video on another old tape. The only thing I couldn't plan was what I was going to say. I didn't know if I would come clean right away about the tape, or if I should play it off like it really happened. I supposed that they would've already shown it if they believed it. They may not want to cause panic if they do, I thought. It was a valid thought, but I waved it away. They didn't seem to be the type to hold information. They like to surprise, quickly.

The thoughts of how it would go down kept me up for a while. I stopped looking at the clock around two in the morning, but it must have been another half hour before I fell asleep.

When my alarm went off, I shot out of bed with no trouble and no desire to return. This is the day, I told myself. I readied myself carefully, but I was set to go long before I'd planned. I made a large breakfast and ate every bite. My stomach complained, but I chalked it up to nerves, and refused to let it slow me down. It told me it wasn't hungry, but I knew it was a liar.

I ended up brushing my teeth again, and being sure to look perfect. It was a strange feeling. Every morning, I would get up and never even glance at the mirror. Today, it felt like the mirror was my only friend, guiding me away from pitfalls.

After waiting and waiting, my ride finally appeared.

Hannah was driving. Jack obviously convinced her to go, but it didn't take much convincing. She knew how to drive to and in the city much better than either Jack or me. She always went there to shop and knew where there was a sixteen-plus club every night. I knew that the second I got out of the car, Hannah would drag Jack around to shop, but it didn't matter to me. I had business to do—business they couldn't help with.

The car ride couldn't end soon enough. I couldn't speak. My brain was muddled, and words didn't come easily. Hannah and Jack conversed—or rather, flirted—throughout the ride, but I could see the silence in the air. It was so thick; you could've spread it on a bagel. The reality was that it wasn't just me going in there for myself. I was going in there for all of us. Our futures could depend on the next few hours.

After agonizing time in rush hour, and a carafe of one ways, Hannah stopped in front of a large, dark building. People were hurriedly rushing in and out, holding briefcases and papers and cups of coffee, just like in the movies. There was a sign with a few different logos on it, but the only one I paid any attention to said, "CNN".

"Ready, dude?" Jack asked. He gave me no look of encouragement.

"No," I grumbled softly. I looked over at Hannah. She gave me a comforting look.

"You'll do good," she consoled. "If not, we have YouTube."

"Yeah! We'll always have YouTube!" Jack added with a grin. "Either way, we'll be famous."

"I guess so." I looked at the clock. It was seven forty-six. "Well, wish me luck," I said as I got out of the car.

Immediately, when I shut the door, I heard Jack yell, "Drive, drive!" I quickly spun around to glare at my so-called-friends. They didn't leave. Jack sat with a pouty look. It lifted me up a little bit. I think that I may have smiled a bit.

"Grow up, Jack," Hannah told him. "Tom, you'll do fine. It'll work." She flashed me a smile. "Right, Jack?" He just muttered under his breath. She rolled her eyes. "Bye." I waved at them as the slowly drove into the turmoil of the city streets. Then, I turned to face my own turmoil.

The building seemed to be growing before my eyes, turning into a gigantic, concrete monster about to eat me whole. People bustled around me, and gave me funny looks for standing there, doing and saying nothing. I took a deep, staggered breath and marched in, trying to look like I belonged there.

The first room was gigantic. It was about the same color as the outside, but it was three times as perfectly shiny. In comparison to the outside, the inside was tame. Sure, there were people bustling here and there, but they were mostly confined to the edges. People patiently waited for the elevators. There was girl at a desk to the right of the room, against the wall. She was talking calmly into her earpiece. Groups of people sat in a few chairs and discussed in a civilized manner. The middle of the room was practically empty.

I went straight to the right side and followed the wall until I reached the desk. I didn't want to disturb the emptiness. It just didn't feel right. The girl at the desk was talking nicely with a smile that said that she actually enjoyed being there. She was blonde, as you'd expect, but she was dressed professionally. Her hair was pulled into a ponytail and she wore glasses with wire frames. Her outfit was black and white and did not reveal anything more than necessary.

I looked at her desk while I waited for her to finish the call. Her name plate was immaculately clean and said, "Keri Holloway". The desk was orderly and sparse. There were only a few papers to be seen, and they were tucked away into a holder. It surprised me when she hung up and looked up at me. "Hi, how can I help you?" she said in a pleasant voice. She smiled at me, and I felt a bit of my nervousness fall away.

"C..." my voice faltered for a second. Apparently, she didn't scare off enough of my nerves. I was sweating buckets. She kept her smile as I tried to fish out my thoughts. I cleared my throat and started again. "CNN?"

She pointed toward the sets of elevators. "Take the elevators up to floor five. Which department are you going to?"

"Umm..." I realized that Linda never told me. "I don't know," I replied.

"Alright, just talk to Linda at their front desk," she said. "Oh, and if you don't like crowds... or just need a little exercise, you can always take the stairs, just around that corner. It won't take you straight to the front, but it shouldn't be too hard to find."

"Thanks," I said and gave her a sheepish, crooked smile.

I decided to take the stairs. I only passed one person. He didn't even look at me. He was too busy talking on his phone. All I heard was, "...the pancakes, and trade them for the camera thing..." Business is weird, I decided.

I took my time getting up the stairs. Unfortunately, it still only took a few minutes. However, it was already seven fifty-three when I reached the door marked with a giant "5" and the CNN logo. The glass was the cloudy kind that lets you know there's something on the other side, but you can't tell whether it's just colorful furniture or a bustling chaos of an office. I could hear a small hum of noise inside, but it was so faint, it couldn't be too busy.

I opened the door and was dead wrong. The door must have been built to be soundproof, because the noise and the disorder inside were truly epic. I stood in the doorway in awe. It was panic. Phones were ringing, and papers were everywhere. People ran around, but the expression on their faces was, without a doubt, the most amazing thing of it all. Most of them held an expression of apathy or boredom, like this happened every day. Which it probably did, I realized.

I stepped inside, and the door closed behind me. I stood close to the door, trying to stay out of everybody's way. People seemed to swerve around me like I was a statue that had been there for months, and everyone was used to it. I didn't move until the door opened behind me and I jumped.

Someone ran into me and I fell over. Everyone around stopped for a second to look, but quickly went back to work. The blood began to rush to my face. I turned to face my attacker. He was about my dad's age—actually; he reminded me a lot of my dad. He had short, dark hair, a suit, a perfectly trimmed beard, and a large, but slightly muscular body. He was about the same height as my dad, and he had the same bushy arched eyebrows. It wasn't my dad, though. This guy's head was a little less circular, and his eyes were brown instead of green. Also, there were little things—eye shape, ear size—that set him apart.

"Thomas!" he bellowed. His voice was a lot deeper than my dad's. "Right on time!" He helped me up and coaxed me down the hall.

"T-tom…" I quietly corrected him. I wasn't sure if he heard me.

The man led me down the hallway with a woman and another man in tow. They were both carrying papers, but he wasn't carrying anything. We arrived at an open door and entered. The woman closed the door, and the noise outside dimmed to a quiet humming that I could easily forget about. The room wasn't large, but it wasn't small. It had a table that could fit about eight people, three on each of the long sides, and one on each of the small sides. There were only five chairs, three on the side closest to the large window, and two on the other side. There was a normal sized television in the corner next to a fake plant. In another corner, there was a filing cabinet. The rest of the room was decorated with framed this, poster that, all having something to do with CNN, I assumed. I didn't take the time to figure out what they were. I couldn't focus on much of anything. I could feel tremors in my hands, as if I hadn't eaten in days, but I know I had.

The lead man and the woman sat down on the side closest to the window. The other man rummaged through the filing cabinet and grabbed a folder. It had a rectangular bulge like there was a miniature tape inside. My tape was inside.

"Thomas, I am Daniel Blake," he introduced in his booming voice. He motioned to the man, then the woman. "This is Derek Cole and Melissa Lund. I am the head of the stories department here in the Minneapolis branch of CNN. These are my associates."

"Tom Grant," I said. They looked at me as if I had something else to say. I really didn't. If I said I was a director, they might assume that I made the whole thing up. I did, but I didn't want to admit it if they didn't know.

Daniel cleared his throat and held his hand out to Derek. Derek placed the folder in his hand, but Daniel didn't even look at it before he spoke again. "All stories around here have to go through me before they can air. Now, of course, your story failed before it got to me," he revealed. My heart stopped beating. Any little tidbit I may have practiced left me then and there. "However, it did end up in my hands before we threw it away or sent you a letter," he continued. "You've got talent, my boy. Someone in the department thought I should see it. Now, I already knew that it was a fake when I started watching. But, if I hadn't known that, I might've believed it."

I sat in silence. I didn't know what he was trying to tell me. I know I probably started fidgeting, but I couldn't tell. The edges of my vision faded out, like I was in a dream, trying to grasp on reality.

"Where did you get the idea for this?" Derek

asked, motioning toward the tape.

"Umm..." My mind was spinning. He was asking me a question. "Well, vampires are...sexy, so...I kinda built off that..." It was incredibly awkward saying the word sexy; it just seemed so unprofessional. Derek just nodded and accepted the answer.

"A brilliant idea," Melissa added. "And, the graphics are superb."

I blushed a little. The compliments were nice, but compliments weren't going to get me on the news.

"It's such a waste to let something like this falter," Daniel admitted. I could tell he was holding something back. He wasn't going to tell me yet. Maybe he's going to get it aired, anyway, I hoped. But, he continued to hold back, smiling with the secret behind his teeth.

I decided to step in, and talk about my dreaded Plan B, just to try and coax it out of him. "Well, I wanted to put it on YouTube, if it didn't work..." I let my voice trail off. I wanted to sound devious or cunning, but it came out as soft and defeated.

"Like I said, waste," Daniel clarified. "Well, we have a plan. But first, tell me, what was your plan with this?"

I was a little startled with the question. I guess I should have expected it, but it never crossed my mind that they would ask. When I didn't respond right away, Melissa piped in, "Were you trying to get rich? Famous?"

"Famous, kinda," I confirmed. "Well, that was mostly Hannah—"

"Which is the girl in the video?" Derek interrupted.

"Yeah, and—"

"How many people are on your team?" Derek interrupted again.

"Four: me, Hannah, Jack, and Alicia," I responded and waited, in case he was going to interrupt me again. He didn't.

"What was Alicia's role in this?" Derek asked.

"She gathered videos and things for me to edit in," I said. She didn't really have a title like Hannah, Jack, and I.

"So, she's the copyright mastermind," Melissa added. I had a quizzical look on my face. She explained, "During the screening process, some people recognized the video...'clips 'that were edited in. Every time they found one, all copyright legalities were taken care of. That girl knows what she's doing."

I knew Alicia was smart, but I never imagined that she would think of even the little things. "Yeah," I agreed, not knowing what else to say.

"So, now we're up to our plan," Daniel interjected. He leaned across the table. "Don't stop here. Send it somewhere else, smaller, local. This time, don't try to trick them. Let them know exactly what's going on. Well, not everything, but that it's a fake. Convince them to air it. Make it believable. We want you to do the leg work. I mean, it is your video." He chuckled. It was a malicious chuckle. I'd barely spoken to him, but I was already beginning to despise him. He had his own agenda.

I pondered it. I wondered if he thought it would work. "So, then what?" I asked.

The three looked at each other. This time, Melissa explained the plan, "If you can get the local channel to run it, then we can run it. Depending on the reaction, we could run it as a hoax. Maybe if we're lucky, we could run it under the impression of it being real." I noticed that she said we and not you. I doubted that I was even included in their "we". No matter where it went, they wanted ratings. They wanted viewers. I was just a pawn.

I would love to say that I, at that point, gained some cunning and played them, but that wasn't the case. I had a chance, and I took it.

"Do you have another copy of this?" Daniel asked, holding up my tape. "I'd like to keep it, in case you succeed."

They didn't think I could do it. I wanted to prove them wrong. "Yeah, it's in my pocket," I replied, trying to keep the ice out of my voice.

"Well, good, I think this was a productive meeting, wouldn't you say so?" Daniel turned to his associates in turn, and they each gave him a professional nod. He turned to me and held out for a handshake. "Thanks for working with us, Thomas."

I plastered on a fake smile and catalogued profanities in my mind. "My pleasure."

"Walk him out, will you, Melissa?" Daniel asked her, and waved me off. I made the conscious decision that I hated him at that point. But, if he was the railroad tracks for my train to success, I suppose I had to buy the ticket.

She said nothing, but stood up and led me to the door. The chaos I'd forgotten about exploded again when she opened the door, and took me by surprise. She kept looking at me like she wanted to tell me something, but she kept her mouth shut until we reached the elevator. We got in and she pressed "L".

We stood there awkwardly until the door closed. It probably would've been more awkward if someone else was there as well, but no one did. The second the doors shut, she said, "He's such an ass."

I just looked at her, in awe of the unprofessional language. She continued, "He didn't want to tell you about the money, but I'll make sure he doesn't forget."

"Huh?" I intelligently said.

"Well," she explained, "you get royalties for the story. He wanted to glaze over it, trying to take advantage of a kid, but I won't let it happen." She pulled out a business card. "If you get your story aired, be sure to call me."

The elevator opened and I stepped out and tried to weave around the people. She didn't get out; she stood there and waited for everyone else to get on with a look of pure contempt on her face. At least I knew that it wasn't aimed at me.

I was left alone in the large room. I kept close to the wall again and made my way outside. I pulled out my phone and dialed Jack. "Hey—" I started.

"I see you," he stated.

"Huh?" Then, I looked straight ahead at the largely-windowed coffee shop across the street. Jack and Hannah were waving. I quickly ran across the street, not bothering with the crosswalk a block away. Luckily, I dodged all of the cars.

I made my way in and heard the door chime as I walked in. The employees watched me as I came in, but were too wrapped up in other customers to linger on my coffee-less presence. I got to the two-chaired table and faced my friends.

"Daredevil," Hannah sarcastically said.

"I know," I said proudly. They waited. "Oh, yeah, I have to tell you guys what happened." I paused again. I grinned and began to tell the story. I decided to leave out the "new plan" and save it, just to be climactic.

"Oh, man," Jack said, looking genuinely sympathetic, "that sucks."

"Wait," Hannah observed, "why are you smiling? What are you not telling us?"

I grinned even wider. "We've got to go

local," I explained.   Then, I filled them in on the new plan, including the part about the royalties.

"Dude!" Jack exclaimed.   "Let's do it!"

CHAPTER SIX

The next day, it was fifty degrees. Compared to before, it was awesome out. Besides that, I was in a great mood, and ready to conquer the world. The plan was in motion, even if it had a few tweaks. I bounded out of bed, and got ready as quick as I could. I felt invincible. I quickly started the car and made my way to school.

Tonight, we'd get the group together and plan. Today, I felt lucky. Today, I was going to ask Alicia out on a date, before the meeting. I couldn't wait for second period. Or first. So, I texted her before school even started.

"hey u free tonite?"

The response was instant. "I can't. I'm sick."

"r u kidding?"

I didn't get a response. That was one way to put a damper on my spirits, but not for long. There would be other days. I pressed on; I was still determined to have a good day. School, like always, got in the way of that. The boredom weighed at me like an anchor. By the end of the day, I just wanted to go home and sleep, but I couldn't. I had work to do.

By eight, I was completely ready to see the group. We were going to need to move quickly; the temperatures were dropping again, and everyone wanted to get home. It had reached about thirty-one degrees by the time everyone got there. Alicia even managed to get out.

"I thought you were sick," I said, not trying to sound accusatory. Obviously, it sounded that way.

"I got better," she said with icicles in every word. Then, she walked right past me, leaving my ego stinging.

I started as soon as everyone settled in the living room.

I held a notebook in my hand. "Alright," I said, taking charge, "we're almost there. Convincing the eleven o'clock news should be easy, but we can't afford any mistakes."

"Did we have any mistakes before?" Jack asked, bored.

"No, but—"

"Then, why do you need to tell us, 'no mistakes'?" he retorted.

"Because we need to succeed," Alicia stated.

I nodded. "Thank you, Alicia. She's right. We need to succeed. Not just to be famous, but to show that asshole, Daniel that we aren't just a bunch of kids." With every passing minute, I felt like a general, giving a pep talk to the troops. It felt good. "We are an intelligent group of talented young adults."

They weren't reacting how I thought they would. They weren't cheering or anything. I probably could have expected that. They were listening to every word, but they weren't energized. At least I knew that they wanted to get Daniel as much as I did. I dove into my new plan of attack on Channel Five.

"So, when are we going to do this?" Jack asked, seemingly a little more excited, probably because I used words like attack, conquer, and destroy. The words were inspired by my feelings toward Daniel. I wished I had the opportunity to squash him like a bug, but the only thing I could do was blow his socks off with my success.

I took a deep breath. "Tomorrow," I answered.

"What?" Hannah exclaimed. "How are we going to pull this off tomorrow?"

"Why tomorrow?" Jack inquired.

"We're running out of time," I explained. "The weather is getting worse, and we'll miss our chance. Today is the exact same weather as the video. It's our window of opportunity. I can feel it!" I could. Although I hadn't been right on the how, I'd been right lately. "We've been given something great, and we can't waste it."

"Come on you guys," Alicia piped in. "It's not that hard. And, he's right, the timing is perfect. Let's get it done!"

Hannah became excited. "Yeah! Let's do it."

Jack was a little more apprehensive. He

looked around. "I don't know…"

"Remember, step one is you missing school for a couple of days…" I enticed. It was a dirty tactic, but I knew Jack would go for it.

His face lit up a bit. "Okay, dude. But, I'm not doing any of the talking tomorrow."

"You won't have to," I said. "Then we'll all meet here tomorrow at nine."

That night, I couldn't sleep for hours. My thoughts were racing around. How's it going to go? Who are we meeting with? What if they don't even see us? What if they say no? The scenarios were playing and playing like I was surrounded by eight televisions on a different channel.

When I did finally sleep, each dream was short, and I woke up incredibly often. First, I was a news anchor with a breaking story about vampires, which looked oddly like Jack. Then, I was at school, and every other girl was Alicia, and I probably kissed about seventy percent of her. Another dream involved me running from a vampire that turned into Hannah, who in turn became a werewolf, a black mess, and the vampire again, and finally, when it caught me, it was Alicia. Her voice was the blaring sound of my alarm.

I bolted out of bed instantly. This was the day that would change my life forever. I was going to get the video to the world. We were going to be famous. I pulled on another dressy outfit and impatiently sat on my couch and waited for everyone to arrive.

They weren't long. Everyone came very early in anticipation. We all sat, fidgeting, and making awkward, choppy conversation. When it came time to go, we all quickly got out of our seats, eager to get going.

We all piled into Hannah's car. The studio for Channel Five was only about ten miles from my house. The car ride was just as awkward as my house. There wasn't any real conversation, and no one could sit still. I held a folder and a DVD in my hand. I kept flipping through the papers, making sure that I had everything. I did. I checked again —I hadn't looked at the papers carefully. I could've printed something out twice and thought it was— no. Everything was there. Did I drop one? When I checked again, I, of course, found that I still had everything.

I began imagining worst-case scenarios again. I was up at the front, and when I put in the DVD, all confident, there was nothing on it. I would probably just run out, no explanation. I started chewing the inside of my lip in anticipation. Suddenly, there was a terribly cold pressure on my hand. I looked over. Alicia had grabbed my hand. Her face, however, was turned out the window, bored. I wanted to say something: ask why her hand was so cold, say thanks, ask if she wanted to go out, or anything at all, but I didn't. I couldn't ruin the moment. I stayed silent, but it wasn't as awkward anymore.

The car slowed to a stop in the parking lot.

It was nine twenty-three. I had called them earlier this morning, telling them that we had a breaking story we'd like to tell. When they asked what it was, I told them it was a secret. They didn't like that too much. I did tell them that we would like to meet with them today. That made it better, but they only guaranteed us ten minutes. That was going to be more than enough time for us.

We all sat in the car for a minute. "Ready?" I asked no one in particular. Actually, I was probably asking myself. The response I got was a couple of nods. The response I got from myself was an increased heartbeat. But nerves keep you on your toes, I told myself.

Slowly, we made our way out of the car. We trudged up to the front door and pressed ourselves inside. I had closed my eyes to prepare for the chaos, but when I opened them, I didn't find it. Everything was much calmer here. There were still a few people rushing, but, for the most part, everything seemed put together already.

I sucked in a nice, deep breath and focused myself. I was now in charge, and I had to believe it. I marched up to the front desk and said, "Tom Grant." My voice did not falter or crack. There was no room for beating around the bush. She directed us down the hall. I knocked on the door. There wasn't a response for a few seconds, but I could hear someone talking inside. Eventually, I heard a deep voice call us in.

This office was small. There was, thank

goodness, a television in the corner. There were exactly enough chairs for all of us, but it was a tight fit. There was only one window, so most of the light was artificial. A lot of the rest of the space was taken up by a large desk with an equally large man sitting behind it. He was talking into the phone in a rushed fashion, but without any physical showing of emotion.

He, out of the blue, hung up the phone. I didn't even recall him saying goodbye or any other conversation-ending phrases. He stared at us in a way that said, "What?" without him having to open his mouth.

I dove right in. "Three days ago, I met with CNN about a tape I sent in a few weeks ago. May I use your television?"

"If you must," he replied, bored.

I played our video for him. This time, watching it, I was empowered. When it finished, I didn't give the man any time to react. He looked at the video and my friends, a bit confused, as I spoke. "I am the director of this video, Tom Grant. These are my actors, Jack and Hannah, and this is my assistant, Alicia. We sent this video to CNN, trying to give them the impression that it was real. We failed instantly. However, they gave me another chance. All you have to do is run this story as if the video was real."

He stared. "And why should I do that?" he asked. I could tell that he was a bit interested, but the presence of my actors, not dead, may have put him off a bit.

I was prepared for that. I opened the folder and took out a few graphs and articles. "These describe the rise of viewers and ratings of news stations who accidentally ran hoaxes," I explained. "As you can see, ratings and viewers skyrocket initially. They ultimately fall at the point of reality." He looked about ready to dismiss us right there, but I continued. "However, the viewer counts fall to a point higher than before and have a higher rate of acceleration later in the game. Besides, CNN has your back.

He looked through them. He began to rise a bit in interest. It wasn't enough. "How do I know these aren't fake?" he asked, still skeptical. "You seem to be pretty good at fakes." He tried to throw it in my face, but I took it as a compliment.

"You don't," I said plainly. "You're just going to have to trust me. Unless you want to look them up yourself." He raised an eyebrow at me.

Alicia cut in. "Are you serious? We have cold hard facts in front of you, and you aren't even going to take the chance?" She stared at him as if she could burn a hole into his eyes. Fiercely, she told him, "Run the story."

A lot of the doubt seemed to rush out of him. He looked through the papers again. "Well, have you taken any social precautions?"

Jack and Hannah looked a little confused, but I knew what he was talking about. "Well, if you run the story soon enough, we won't need much more than we've already done."

He thought for a moment. "How about tonight on the five o'clock news?"

I was in control here. "I think that this more of a breaking story, don't you think?" I quipped.

He looked at me sternly. "I don't think the network could afford you to interrupt our programming," he explained. I wanted to strangle him. It would never work as a normal story. No one would believe it if it were played as any old news story.

"Why not 'interrupt 'the news?" Hannah quietly suggested.

I looked at her and just wanted to hug her. She was a genius. Underneath the blonde hair and shallow heart was a mind.

He gave us a quizzical look. "I guess I could do that," he admitted.

The rest of the conversation was a blur. He was going to run the story. That also meant that CNN was going to run the story. I was absolutely sure that my dad could forgive the broken window he was going to see when he got home.

We returned to my house for a free day. Hannah and Jack kept their faces covered. I know that my neighbors might recognize them anyway, but I thought that they would mostly be at work anyway. I got in and covered the broken window with saran-wrap, at least. I made sure that all of the curtains and blinds were closed so no one could look in. We kind of did a lazy job; Hannah and Jack's cars were here, people probably saw them, and there were other small clues, like how Hannah went out in the sun all the time, but it didn't matter too much. We weren't expecting to keep the charade up forever.

My dad arrived home at about four thirty. The first thing he said, surprisingly calm, "Tom, um, what happened to the window?"

I decided to take it slow. "Yeah, I kinda broke it. But, I covered it," I pointed out.

"I see that." He looked at the excited bunch of chattering teenagers. "Are we having a party for the broken window, or a broken window for the party?"

He was still trying to be cool, even if I was in big trouble. "No," I said, "but in about a half hour, you'll see why."

He sighed. "Alright, whatever." Jack gave me a thumbs-up. I returned it. My dad rolled his eyes and got a soda. He sat on the couch and stared at us expectantly. "So, what is it?" he asked.

"You'll find out," I said mysteriously. Alicia rolled her eyes, and Hannah giggled. Then, we all sat in silence. For us teenagers, it was a happy, excited silence. For my dad, I was guessing that it was an annoyed, you're-very-grounded-when-your-friends-go-home silence. I was amazed that he didn't figure out what was going on. I'd told him about the plan, but he probably didn't believe it.

I decided that this was a celebration. I

turned on some music. I grabbed a few bags of chips and some more sodas. We were all talking excitedly, being very careful not to give it away. I wanted to see the look on my dad's face when he saw my work. Before we knew it, it was five o'clock. I quickly turned off the music and took a seat next to my dad. I looked at him and he ruffled my hair. I relaxed a little bit, and hoped the window was forgotten already.

The news anchors greeted Minnesota and shared some playful banter. Everyone, except for my dad, was enraptured in the screen. He sat on the couch, bored. He wouldn't be bored for long. "So, wait, what did you guys do to get on the news?" he asked, mildly concerned. "You didn't rob a bank, did you?" He sounded joking, but I could tell in his tone that he was afraid that we'd done something especially bad.

I shushed him. "You'll see!" I exclaimed.

The news went on with its boring stories: the weather report, an apartment fire, and a new charity. They were in the middle of announcing what product was "sweeping the nation" in popularity, when the anchorwoman stopped mid-sentence and began reading something just off of the camera.

Everyone held their breath. This was the moment. My heart was beating more and more quickly with every passing second. Then, the woman spoke.

"We have a breaking story here at Channel

5. We will break to an important clip." Then, after a second of flashing thoughts of failure, it was our movie.

Of course, it started with the porn. I looked at my dad and his wide eyes. I blushed. That isn't normally something you wanted your dad to see. Then, it transitioned to the violence and terror and his face turned to complete disgust. I never knew he couldn't handle gore very well.

The anchorman started talking. "This is unbelievable. Considering the circumstances, the U.S. government currently has no course of action. Here at Channel Five, we urge you to stay indoors and continue watching for our new segment, Vampire Watch."

They continued to talk, and Jack's, Hannah's, and Alicia's eyes stayed glued on the screen. Jack's and Hannah's phones were exploding for the time being, but they knew to ignore them for now. I looked at my dad. He was speechless.

"You actually did it," he finally spat out. "I-I can't believe it. You made that?" I nodded excitedly. "I'm going to go...lie down." He got up and trudged towards his room like he was drunk.

We all began cheering, not caring who heard. We'd done it.

"Quick, turn to CNN!" Alicia shouted.

I fumbled around for the remote until I found it. I quickly changed to CNN. They were just starting a new report.

"…real vampires. Here's that chilling video." Our clip was shown again on television. It was surreal.

My phone rang. I looked at the caller ID. I remembered a number like that. It looked oddly like the number CNN used to call me with. I knew that I had to answer it.

"Hello?" I answered.

"Good job, kid," Daniel responded on the other end. "You're famous." He disconnected.

I smiled. Even though he seemingly won, I know that I was the real winner. Famous… I thought. Alicia was flipping through the channels. They all seemed to be jumping on the bandwagon. One was showing the end of the video. I saw myself looking into the camera, terrified. I swore that they kept it there for an extra second. The anchor said something, but all I could pick out was "…Thomas Grant."

Daniel's words rang in my head again. You're famous. I was about to become a poster child for vampire attacks. I wouldn't be surprised if they were on their way to start knocking on my door. I was the survivor. I looked around at my group. They were all having a good time. I hated to ruin it, but…

"We have to get out of here," I stated. I couldn't believe I hadn't thought of it before. I peered outside discretely. No one was there yet, but I was ready to run. I could imagine the neighbors seeing the broken window, confirming the story, and rushing over.

"What?" Jack said.

"Everyone is going to come after me," I said, looking around. "We've got to go."

Jack groaned.

Hannah said, "He's right. We can hide at my house."

"We can't. You're supposed to be dead and a vampire. People are going to be busting down your door, too," Alicia explained. She took a deep breath and continued, "Let's go to my house."

I shrugged. "Works for me; we just gotta go."

We quickly grabbed a few things: chips, music, soda, and clothes. Then, we headed out. "Whose car are we taking?" I asked no one specific.

"Mine," Alicia said without missing a beat or even looking at anyone. She climbed into her car and started it. We all jumped in, and, before we could even settle into our seats, she sped off. She couldn't have been obeying speed limits or other pesky street laws. None of us got the chance to figure out where we were going. All I know is that she lived on the outskirts in some little township.

We arrived at her house. It was a small, brown house, and it had no neighbors. However, what it lacked in size and friendliness, it more than made up for in trees. You could probably commit murder at this house, and no one would know.

CHAPTER SEVEN

"Are you sure your parents won't mind if we stay for the night, or even a couple nights?" I asked before we reached the front door. We trudged on the cold ground. The pathway was all dirt, but it felt like cement in the cold.

"They're gone," she replied. She arrived at the door and opened it without unlocking it.

"You don't lock your doors?" Jack inquired. Our city wasn't a bad city, but everyone knew to lock their doors. You never knew who was going to come by.

"No," Alicia responded. "I don't think anyone will break in here. Besides, my sister's here." She hadn't looked at us since we left my house.

I walked in and shivered. "It's freezing in here." I rubbed my hands on my arms, hoping to warm up a bit, but it didn't really help. I could've sworn it was colder inside than it was outside.

"Heater's broken," she explained. She instantly made a beeline down the hall before we could follow. Jack, Hannah, and I shared puzzled looks. She had walked into a door and was talking to someone. I could hear her talk, but I couldn't understand what they were conversing about. She almost sounded really angry. I couldn't see anything she could've been angry about already, but I guessed I'd never seen the house before. Alicia emerged from the door a minute later, but shut it before we could look at the other participant.

"Who were you talking to?" I dared to ask.

"My sister, Angela," she replied quickly. She was acting incredibly odd. Alicia, the girl who always maintained the I-own-the-world attitude was suddenly jumpy. She darted her eyes around, watching us look around the room.

"Do we get to meet her?" Hannah politely asked. She was always so friendly.

Alicia, however, wasn't. She started muttering things under her breath—things that sounded a lot like profanity. "She'll come out eventually," she responded quietly. Hannah looked a little hurt. Alicia looked a little hurt herself, but not in the same way. She looked vulnerable. Had it not been for that, I might've said something.

"So, this is my house," she said awkwardly. "Don't go exploring too much." She paused for a moment while we contemplated the words. "Er, my parents, they always know when people snoop around." I'd never given much thought to what Alicia's parents were like. She seemed so independent. Sometimes, I think my mind assumed she didn't need any.

I actually looked around the house for the first time. The walls were a light blue, artistic, cool color. The high parts of the walls were completely covered with art from almost every time period and every country. It seemed impossible that so much culture could fit in an area that came at least two feet from the floor. I hadn't noticed before, because the blue paint was so light, that there was a white design crawling up from the floor, up to the tip of the picture frames.

Against the wall was a massive music... I wasn't sure what to call it. It had a place for CDs, cassette tapes, and eight tracks. It also had a place for records, iPods, MP3 players, radios, and any other musical medium. Against it was an electric guitar. Although I didn't know much about guitars, it definitely looked like a nice one.

As if I had no control over the movement of my eyes, they were led further on to the television. It wasn't huge, but it was nice. It was a flat screen that was black. It wasn't a dark or dull grey like you saw on most televisions, but it was like the television was still on when it was off. Next to it was the movie collection. I meandered in its direction like a zombie. Movies were like my crack-cocaine. I put my fingers over the titles: The Princess Bride, The Notebook, How to Lose a Guy in 10 Days... They were all incredibly sappy movies. Some may have been humorous, but they all were the kind of movies where men stopped a plane or traveled across the country for the girl.

These were the movies that made women hit their boyfriends for not being romantic.

"Wow," I accidently muttered. It was a reflex.

"We really like art," Alicia explained. She faced another direction, not realizing that I was talking about the movies. It was a vast collection. I looked over at her. She was staring at Hannah who'd begun tracing the wall, looking at all of the different forms of art. With every step she took, Alicia got more and more tense. I was afraid she would pounce if Hannah reached a door.

"You sure do," Jack said. "Your family is very..." Jack struggled with the words. He never had a giant vocabulary.

"Cultured," I finished.

"Yeah," he agreed.

"Yeah, our family is very cultured," said a young voice very smugly. She said cultured like it was some kind of joke.

I looked toward the sound of the voice. It came from a girl standing right behind Hannah. She looked about seventeen, Alicia's age. They didn't look too much alike. They must have had one different parent. Angela was also average height, and definitely had some Asian blood in her as well. However, her skin was much paler than Alicia's. Her hair was also long and black, but Angela's was a bit wavy, obviously naturally. Angela wore much louder makeup than Alicia, and she impossibly wore a short skirt and a shirt that didn't quite cover her midriff.

"This is Angela," Alicia introduced grudgingly.

Jack stared at this new girl. Angela stared right back with her smug smile still on her face. Jack held out a hand for her to shake. "Jack," he explained.

She took his hand and shook it. The smile was almost sinister. It gave me a chill down my spine. Then, she spoke again in her haughty voice. "This is the company you keep around?" she asked Alicia in almost a laugh. Alicia stared her down. It was like fire was coming from her eyes. Angela continued, "Whatever. Not my choice of friends."

"Why haven't I seen you in school?" Hannah asked.

Angela tore her attention away from Jack and Alicia. She held a different look on her face than she did with Jack. To her, Jack was like something she would devour. She held herself like one of those girls who took a boy, took his life and his money, and then dumped him on the side of the road with nothing but a broken life and a broken heart. When she looked at Hannah, she was like competition. Angela had a look in her eye that said she'd like nothing more than to rip out Hannah's heart.

Angela opened her mouth, and I had a sharp intake of breath. When Angela's smile faded, I knew that nothing good was going to come out of that mouth. Luckily, Alicia's mouth was quicker.

"She's homeschooled."

Angela raised an eyebrow at Alicia. "Yeah," she explained. "They can't handle me at public schools, private schools, military schools..." A burst of pride flashed through her face. "So, our parents have to teach me." Angela must've had no respect for her parents. It almost disgusted me. However, I still wondered how a child could've become like that.

"Leave, Angela," Alicia ordered. She wasn't loud, and she didn't growl. Her voice, though, was stern, and it was almost as if her word wasn't just an order or a rule. It was law.

Had I been in that position, I would've probably looked down and left. Angela merely laughed. "Alright, sis. I have to go play hockey with some boys, anyway." She walked right past us, without grabbing any gear, or even any warm clothes. While she had nice legs, it was suicide to walk out dressed like that. The second she opened the door, I expected her to shiver or curse, theatrics ruined. She didn't. She walked outside like it was a nice summer morning, started a car, and left.

"Whoa," Hannah finally said.

"I hate her," Alicia said. "I'm not sure why I try."

I gave her a confused look. "That's not really up to you, is it? She's your sister," I pointed out.

"I guess so," she responded. She was

fuming inside, I could tell, but she tried her hardest to keep it under control.

We all stood uncomfortably for quite a few minutes until Jack finally said, "So, now what do we do?" I shot Jack a dirty look. He knew nothing of tact.

"Right," Alicia realized out loud. She reached for a remote and turned on the magic television.

I instantly had to take a seat. It really was magical. I'd seen high definition before, but this was higher definition. It was like the picture was physical, pushing onto my eyes, making them dry.

"Where did you get a TV like this?" Hannah exclaimed. Although the sound wasn't loud, it felt like it, causing us to raise our voices.

Alicia paused. "My dad—he built it. There's no other one like it." She said it like it was no big deal, but it was.

We were all speechless. I didn't even know what was on, but I could feel the light particles coming out of the television. The sound was all around. I saw no speakers, but I heard it. It was creeping out of the walls, like a snake. I could almost see it slither out of the corners.

"...Stay on watch," I finally registered a reporter saying. Alicia was sitting on a couch, enraptured in the story, and not in the graphics or the sound. It was hard to keep my mind focused on the story. My mind kept breaking off its thoughts to enjoy the pictures and lights and sounds... "...

news, a fire..." I felt like a little thread above my eyebrows was beginning to unravel itself...

I rapidly began turning my head, looking for an escape. I saw an open room, dove into it, and slammed the door. The sound dulled and the lights were abruptly taken from me. Apparently, I had been sweating. I left the lights off, not wanting any recollection of the explosion of lights and colors.

It left me panting. I could hear the television still going, but I couldn't risk going back. I heard yelling. The sound of the television quickly stopped. The screaming began to die down.

"I forgot," I heard Alicia explain. "It's a lot to get used to."

I kept my back against the door. It was nice and cold. I never knew that, especially this year, I'd ever welcome the cold, but I welcomed it and let it embrace me. I slid to the floor and sat on the even colder tile floor, letting it seep into my jeans, calming my breathing.

When my eyes finally adjusted to the darkness, I took a look around. I couldn't see much, but I noticed the cabinet underneath the sink was open. I slugged my way over to it, even though nothing under a sink had ever caught my attention.

There was a giant collection of cleaners. That wasn't so out of the ordinary, except there were so many. There were at least eight different floor cleaners. Some of them were industrial-strength cleaners you couldn't get at an average store. I saw two with labels in a foreign language. All of them were open, and many were less than half full. I couldn't imagine the need for so many cleaners in such a small household. Besides that, they had only lived here for two years or so.

Gaining some strength, I was able to stand and turn the lights on. Instantly, I squinted, and it hurt my head a little bit, but it subsided after a few seconds. I looked around the bathroom in a new light. It didn't look like it was cleaned every twelve seconds. If it was, it must get dirty very often. There was dirt in nearly every crack and the mortar between the floor tiles was a terrible shade of reddish-brown in some places.

I took the time to splash water on my face and regain my composure. When I looked in the mirror right over the sink, my face was red and my eyes were bloodshot. It was either like I'd just run a marathon, or that I'd just witnessed a murder.

I stared into the mirror until my own image was burned permanently into my subconscious. After several minutes, I finally opened the door. I took a minute at the doorway and took a quick visual sweep of the house. Everything was clean, but nothing was immaculately clean, like the cleaners would have you believe. I didn't know if it were the fact that Alicia's parents were gone—for who knows how long—or if the cleaners were left from a previous owner. However, it stuck there in my mind, like a tick, sucking out bits of my coherent thoughts.

I slipped out of the bathroom and rejoined my friends. Jack had his eyes closed and was rubbing his temples. Alicia was in her kitchen getting water. Hannah was shaking a bit, but she seemed otherwise fine.

"Something crazy, right?" I asked Jack and Hannah. I gave them a sheepish smile.

Hannah nodded. Jack ignored me. Alicia came back with water for them both. She turned to me. "Do you need some?" she asked.

At the mention of it, my throat became dry and my lips seemed to crack on cue. "Yeah," I replied quietly.

She quickly returned with some water. Her face seemed to transform to expressionless—more and more by the second. I wondered what time it was. I looked around for a clock or a window. I found a clock, but in my searching, I'd realized that there were no windows.

"You don't have any windows," I pointed out.

"You just noticed?" Jack said—eyes still closed.

I couldn't believe I never noticed it before. It was such a normal thing that I guess it didn't even cross my mind.

"My parents," Alicia explained, "they think that the sun will fade our walls and our floors."

"Dude," Jack stated, finally opening his eyes,

"there's something wrong with your parents."

"Yeah, you should have seen all those cleaning supplies in the bathroom. If anything is going to fade the paint, it's that," I agreed.

Alicia gave a quivering laugh. I looked at her. She was really starting to look nervous. It was so unlike her. In one moment, she regained herself and wiped all emotion from her face. I almost felt like she should've been the vampire instead of Hannah. While Hannah may have done a fantastic job, she was like an open book. You could see her emotions like they were written in bold print. With Alicia, she was like a white wall in seconds. I bet she could've painted on any face she wanted to. Then, I realized, she probably did every day. I wondered what she really thought every day.

She tried to nonchalantly sidle to the bathroom. I pretended not to notice.

When she emerged, she held three blankets and five or six pillows. "It's getting late," Alicia stated, back to her emotionless stare. "You guys should go to bed." She threw the blankets and pillows on the floor.

I raised an eyebrow. "What about you?" I asked.

"I am sleeping in my room," she said and stalked off to that very room, shutting the door a bit too loudly.

I stared. Sometimes, she was so unbelievably cool, but sometimes, she was a real snob.

"Wow," Hannah said, "way to be a bitch." Jack snickered.

I shot her a look. I'm not one-hundred percent sure what the look said. I know that I wanted to sympathize with Alicia, not just because I had a gigantic crush on her, but also because we were the ones in her space, and I can't imagine that it's easy to be a host—well, for someone like her, anyway. At the same time, I definitely agreed with Hannah. Alicia was acting like a stuck-up bitch.

I didn't know why I liked her so much. She held herself above everyone else. She was cold and distant. But, I knew that it was a mask. If only I could remove the façade, I knew that what was underneath would be beautiful. It had to be.

Jack, Hannah, and I shuffled the blankets and things around in order to get comfortable. I ended up on the couch while Jack and Hannah were on the floor. They weren't close, but they weren't so far apart that they couldn't slide together seemingly unnoticed in the middle of the night. I really hoped that they wouldn't, but it definitely wouldn't be the first time.

It couldn't have been longer than mere minutes before my ears were soothed with the sound of deep breaths from both Hannah and Jack. I was still wide awake. I didn't see how they could sleep. My mind was reeling. I rethought about our story, how it was going to change our lives, what people would say when they found out it was fake, and the trouble the news companies could get in. I also thought about Alicia—her sister, the cleaners, her emotionless expression, and that hot, hot body.

Once my mind got to Alicia, it stayed there. I could imagine bringing my hand up the curves of her arm as she held me in a loving embrace. I imagined how it would feel to kiss that perfect set of lips as we were intertwined.

It took a loud snore from Jack to jog me out of my imagination. I looked at Jack and Hannah. They hadn't moved. They looked the same as they always had. Hannah looked peaceful and perfect. Jack was sprawled out in all directions. And they were close; they were always close.

But I'd changed their lives forever. While they may have looked the same, and probably thought the same, everything would change. Everything had changed. Their lives, even if they weren't currently living them, were now drastically different than when they woke up that morning. Right now, everyone thought that they were dead. There were probably people crying, people confused. Where does everyone think I am? I thought. I wondered if anyone knew where Alicia lived. As far as I knew, we were her only friends. Her sister might rat us out though... I wondered if it was something she would do.

Maybe it's better if she does, I thought. The charade, as short as it was, had gone far enough. We'd tricked the world already, but what were the repercussions? There may have been people quitting their jobs and running away. Some people could've boarded themselves up, vowing never to go to the surface. People could've killed themselves. I tried not to think about it, but it was true. But, I wondered why the stations would do it. They were the responsible adults, and we were the dumb kids. We may have been responsible for so much, and they helped us along. Why?

There was so much I wondered about, so much I didn't know. My head spun in circles that ran too fast for my consciousness to comprehend. I wanted to scream. Had I opened my mouth, I might've. I kept it shut as tightly as I could. I quietly sat up on the couch. I looked around the dark room. There was a light under Alicia's door. I crept up and sneaked to her door. I rapped on the door silently. The door opened just a little.

"What do you want, Tom?" Alicia asked, annoyed, from the other side.

"Just to talk," I responded. "I can't sleep." I almost turned around then, ready to fall into the couch again, unable to sleep.

Before I could head back, I heard a sigh. She opened the door and pulled me in, closing the door behind me quickly. She sat down on the bed, and I stood where she deposited me near the door. I looked around her room. It was the same as the main room, but it was chromatically opposite. The walls were crimson with a black design. The portraits and paintings were Gothic Central. It wasn't mainstream goth, with heavy metal and chains. It was more like a Victorian goth—filled with dark Romanticism and old magic.

"Are you going to stand there, or are we going to talk?" she asked impatiently. I could hear my mind saying all of these awful things that had built up about her bitchiness, but I could never say things like that—especially not to her.

"Sorry," I mumbled and added something about not wanting to bother her. I continued, "Nice room." I tried to sound louder, but it came out still a bit shaky.

She looked around it proudly and said, "I know."

After that, we sat in awkward silence, as was customary for me. She waited, expectantly. I opened my mouth to say something but nothing seemed to come out. I didn't know what to say. I always didn't know. At that moment, as if it had a mind of its own, my hand began to drift toward hers. The few inches seemed like miles until it finally touched her cold, soft skin. She let out a small, stuttering gasp. I looked at her. She was the most beautiful thing I had ever seen. In an instant, her icy hand was metaphorically on fire and her skin was dragging me into its hypnotic spell. I leaned in closer and Alicia tensed up.

I quickly closed the distance before I could change my mind or Alicia could slap me. Her lips were soft and inviting, but made cold by the frigid air around us. I meant to pull away, but I didn't. I began kissing her harder, and suddenly something in her snapped. She started to kiss me back, harder than I had been kissing her. My hands began to trail up her body. When did my hands get up her shirt? I reflected. Every part of my body was burning and freezing all at once.

I was lost in the moment. There was a fleeting thought at the back of my head that I should get back, before she strikes me, but it never took a real hold on me. I could just feel the parts of her skin on my own.

Unexpectedly, there was a loud knock on the door, and I was quickly brought to reality. My hands still longed for her body, but I reluctantly pulled my clothes on. I didn't even remember taking them off. Luckily, I was still in my underwear, but I was still instantly embarrassed. Alicia was muttering profanity.

"Yeah?" I croaked.

"You guys have to get out here!" Hannah yelled worriedly.

I ran to the door and wrenched it open. "Why?" I asked. "What's wrong?"

She held up her little television that I desperately wish I had. She explained, "There's another video."

CHAPTER EIGHT

"What do you mean, 'another video'?" I demanded, not moving from the spot.

"Look!" she ordered.

On her little television, all I could see was a forest and some kids running and screaming. It looked like a Grade-B, or even a Grade-C, horror movie. I gave Hannah a questioning look. She looked at the little television again and whispered, "Shit." She flipped through the channels, but apparently couldn't find what she was looking for.

She groaned. "So, anyway, I got up to watch this...thing...that was only on tonight at three o'clock, but when I turned on my TV, it was still on CNN, so I watched it a while. They introduced this new video. It shows these kids running from a vampire and it kills most of them. It looked as real as ours did," she explained. She stuttered at the word, thing, but I knew that I couldn't dwell on that now.

"Did they say where it was from?" I asked.

"No." Even though it may not have necessarily been from Minnesota, I knew that this was Daniel's doing. Deep down, I knew he was playing us. I didn't know how another video was going to screw us over, but I knew that Daniel was the bad guy here.

"Flip through other channels," I commanded. I strode to the main room to find Jack still sleeping. I kicked him lightly. "Get up," I said, not even looking at him. He grumbled something I couldn't understand. "You idiot," I said quietly.

"Tom, hurry!" Hannah exclaimed. I raced back to where I had left her. Hannah and I huddled around the little television. I couldn't help but notice how warm she was, in comparison to how cold I had been, standing in the freezing cold without a blanket like her.

"...haunting videos," was all I caught before they began playing the clip. It was a highlight reel of our video. Hannah let out a groan of frustration. Then, they began playing another video. This looked like another highlight reel, only it wasn't our video. It was in a forest, and kids were screaming and running. The thing chasing them looked so human, but its expression was pure animal. I watched as he tore off someone's head, and as he bit someone's neck. This video was good.

"This video is almost as good as ours," I said. It was the truth—nearly. It was as good; it may have even surpassed ours. CNN was looking for ratings, and now, they were definitely going to get them.

I needed to talk to Daniel now. "What time

is it?" I asked no one specific.

"Too early," replied Jack, rubbing his eyes. I glared at him, even though he probably had no idea what was going on.

I looked around for the clock. It was about three-fifteen in the morning. I almost didn't believe it. Without the presence of windows, it could've been any time. It could've even been three-fifteen in the afternoon, but that didn't make any sense at all. Even three-fifteen in the morning seemed to be a bit late. I must've slept some, even though it didn't feel like any time had passed at all.

"We have to talk to Daniel," I stated, as if I were in charge. I guessed I was, but it didn't feel like it. "Jack, you stay here with Alicia. Hannah, come drive me to CNN."

They looked at me like I was crazy, but it didn't matter. This was our time to shine, and if Daniel got in the way of that, we would take him down, by any means we could.

Hannah spoke up. "What makes you think that he'll be there?"

I didn't need to think. I was charged. "Nothing," I replied. "But, we can wait there until he is. We need to be there. We need to confront him for the dirty scumbag he is."

I saw a little bit of agreement in their faces, and I took it. I walked straight to the door, and Hannah silently followed. I threw open the door without even a small goodbye.

I strode outside and shut the door, ready to go. Instantly, I registered how warm it was. It was warmer than the inside of Alicia's house. I couldn't help but feel sorry for her, having to live in that cold house all the time.

I started walking, but it didn't take long for me to recognize that I had no destination. The driveway only had one car, and it wasn't Hannah's,

I uttered, "Fuck."

"Oh, it's fine. I'll call one of the guys," She said and pulled out her phone. I meant to give her a perplexed look, but she wasn't paying attention. "...yeah, down on 32nd Street. Yes, there's a house there. Forget speed limits. You know that we can pay for the ticket. Okay." She shut the phone.

If she has chauffeurs, I thought, why would she bother driving herself? I wasn't complaining, but Hannah always kept me guessing. Although she was one of my best—and, I guess, one of my only—friends, I'd written her off as a shallow, spoiled, air-headed girl. I never really stopped to notice these bits and pieces of her, needing to keep my distance from my best friend's girl.

My mind pushed the thoughts away, driving me to act on the task in front of me. "How long will it be?" I asked impatiently.

"Well, Carl isn't much of a fast driver, and he's the only one available. But, he always wants to impress us, so probably about five minutes," she explained.

We waited outside for about five minutes.

Hannah and I didn't talk the whole time. But I did think about us talking. Every time her and Jack broke up, we'd spend more time together. It never lasted, but it was nice. It was like Jack's personality took hold of her and molded her into someone else. When we talked when we were alone, she was perceptive and, although I never realized it until now, she was smarter. We could've talked about the perplexity of Alicia's family, or the cause for her bipolar demeanor tonight, but we were silent.

Hannah was right; within the silent five minutes, a nice, shiny black Mercedes pulled up. I climbed into the backseat, and Hannah followed. A man—young, blonde, muscled—turned around in the driver's seat. "Where are we off to? Home?" he inquired.

"Yep," Hannah said before I could open my mouth. I shot her an angry glare. As Carl pulled out of the driveway, Hannah turned to me. "I need to let my parents know I'm okay. Plus, you're in no condition for the meeting," she commented. She told Carl, "Make sure we aren't seen." He nodded.

I was a bit shocked. So far, I'd been the only one fully into this plan. When she did something as simple as telling her driver not to be seen, I realized that she may have been just as preoccupied with this as I was, just in a different way.

I tried not to, but eventually, I looked down at myself. My clothes were wrinkled and grungy. I was sure that my hair was a mess, and I just looked terrible. She was right; I needed a change of clothes—if not a change of skin.

Hannah kept urging Carl to go faster. The speedometer surpassed one hundred a few times. It was amazing that we weren't in an accident. We were pulling into a gated driveway within three or four minutes. The car drove into a garage attached to a very large house covered in darkness. I didn't even get a chance to look at it before we were already encased inside.

"Thanks, Carl," Hannah said, and she grabbed my hand to pull me out of the car. She carried me along quickly, before I could grasp any of the many rooms we passed through. When we arrived at what I assumed was Hannah's room, she let go of my hand and scurried off the second she turned on the light. I gasped. The room was bigger than my house. The walls were neon blue with not much on them. There was a poster or two on each wall with a punk band or singer on them. I saw a large television that could have held six of my own. Attached to it were every current console, a DVD player, a cable box, a sound system, and a few black boxes I didn't recognize. There were multiple doors and a few drawers built into the walls. There were about eight different comfortable chairs in bright colors and a large white couch. Of course, there was also a bed larger than my dad's.

What really got me was how bare it seemed. Of course, the room was worth more money than all of my dad's possessions, but there was so little inside the room, it felt like no one lived in there. Jack's room held a similar look to my own, with clothes thrown around everywhere, tables filled with cheap, meaningless things, and garbage cans overflowing. Alicia's room was clean, but it too had a lot of stuff—not that I spent a lot of time studying her room. Every space seemed to be a home for something. Hannah's room wasn't like that. I'm sure there was plenty of stuff in her closet and her drawers, but it was almost like a hotel room, being stayed in for a week or so.

Hannah emerged from one of the doors with some clothes on hangers. She thrust them into my hands. She pointed at a door and said, "Take a shower in there and change. I'll be done before you are, so then we can adjust if we need to."

I cautiously entered the bathroom, preparing for something chrome and expensive and extravagant. Thankfully, it seemed normal, to an extent. Everything was white or a dark blue. Everything was pristinely clean, and I felt as if my very presence was attracting dirt to the blank walls. This bathroom definitely seemed like the true home of the cleaning supplies in Alicia's house.

I carefully turned on the shower, using the shiny knobs lightly, trying not to smudge them or leave any clue that I'd been there. I jumped into the water and let the hot liquid run down my body, pulling out any knots that were beginning to tighten under my skin. It felt incredibly relaxing, and I could feel my eyelids get the slightest bit heavier as my thoughts began to calm down a bit. I was finally able to simmer to a point of enjoying the shower. I scanned the array of soaps, unable to tell the function of any of them with a quick glance. I picked the first soap that said shampoo and poured it on my hair. I lathered it through and was surprised at how gritty it had gotten. It felt so cleansing, and I could feel some of the negative energy flow from my head. I didn't believe in that "energy" garbage, but it sure felt like it. I picked another soap, and read body wash somewhere on it. I spread it all over my body quickly and began to rinse it off. The second it left my skin, it began to tingle, and I almost put it on again, just to feel it longer. Before I could make that decision, my brain finally held back to reality and the task I needed to accomplish.

I quickly jumped out of the shower and took a towel from the rack. I dried off as rapidly as I could and began to pull on the clothes. My fingers snagged on the shirt's tag. I hadn't realized I'd be the first one wearing these clothes. I almost wondered why Hannah had them, but with so much money, I just thought, *Why not?* The tag was ultimately ripped off in the struggle. I picked it up from the floor and looked at it. I gasped, "Holy shit." The number was larger than three of my old paychecks, back when I worked at a coffee shop. That was just the shirt. I immediately ripped the tags off all of the clothes and threw them away without focusing on any number.

I looked in the mirror. My hair was still a bit wet and its curls hung heavy and low, like they always did before they dried. The bags under my eyes seemed to minimize a bit after the wash, but were ultimately still there, visibly. However, the clothes were a sight to see. I'd never worn—or even held—any clothes so expensive in my life. But I knew why they were so much. I looked incredibly good. I actually looked like I had taste, and I had power. I looked older. I looked strong. They fit me well, and, to be perfectly honest, I longed to have them every day of my life.

I tore myself away from my own new image and stepped out of the bathroom. Hannah wasn't back yet. I longed to go exploring in that house. Besides raging parties, I never got to see how the richer people lived. Ignoring any cautioning thoughts, I opened the door a crack and tiptoed into the hallway. It was dark in the hallway, just like every other room. I didn't dare turn on a light; for fear that I may be seen.

I had only taken a few steps down the hallway when I could hear Hannah's voice not much farther. "...letting you guys know I'm okay," she said. I followed it a bit and saw a bit of light poking out from one of the collection of doors. In the dim light, I saw a silhouette of someone shadowed on the wall. I recognized the figure and assumed it to be Hannah, standing inside the room, but obviously still at the door.

"Okay?" a deep voice said, bored.

"You woke us up for that?" asked a shrill, important-sounding voice. Those must be her parents, I deduced.

"W-well, I—" Hannah stammered.

"I'm going back to bed," replied the shrill voice. The other voice just grunted, and they both went silent.

Hannah walked out of the room and silently closed the door. I couldn't see her face, but I knew from her ragged breathing that she was on the verge of crying. I felt my way to her and put an arm around her shoulder. She didn't start crying, but it took a while for her breathing to become normal.

I led her back to her room, surprisingly. I couldn't believe I picked the right door. I felt like an idiot for closing it earlier, but I got lucky, so it didn't matter. Hannah finally began to breathe normally and quietly remarked, "They don't even care. All they care about is their stupid money and their stupid stuff, and…" Her voice quavered before it died. She started again, "They've probably never seen the video. They've probably never even seen me in daylight. For all they know, the video is true." She sniffled. I gave a comforting rub on her arm.

She stood up and shuffled to her bathroom. After a few minutes, she emerged back into the dim room. "Push the button on the wall next to you," she told me. I pushed it. There was a loud rolling sound. I looked around. Hannah had large metal covers on her windows used to keep the sun out. The sun was just beginning to rise. It was hard to comprehend that it was already the next day.

"Come on," she said. "I can't stay in this room too long." She got up slowly, but walked quickly toward the door. Her head didn't turn or wander to look at anything like I did. She stared straight at the frame, like it were her last hope.

I followed behind her, a bit slower. I looked around at everything. My gaze never lingered on anything—being sure not to miss anything—until I passed the mirror right next to the door. I stopped at it. I really took a look in the mirror, and I didn't recognize who I saw. I looked older, twenty, maybe. I actually looked like I had somewhere to be, and my time was important. I didn't look like a boy playing dress-up or a nervous guy on his first interview. I wasn't a boy anymore. I had turned my world upside-down, and I was finally taking charge.

Hannah appeared behind me and said, "Tom…"

I turned to her and looked at her—really looked at her, for the first time in years. She was wearing formal, expensive, sexy secretary wear. It was dark grey and made sure to touch on every curve. It showed just the right amount of skin, and exposed her fashion sense to its true colors. She didn't look like the girl I'd known for a decade or so. She looked like a woman. She looked beautiful.

She stood behind me. We stood there, still as marble statues for minutes upon minutes. We didn't appear to be just teenage friends, or anything of the sort. I didn't feel like I was looking in a mirror. I saw a magazine—financial or political. We were plastered on the front cover, frozen and sexy. Our eyes were filled with fire and purpose, but without a wrinkle in sight. We bore into everyone's skulls like a needle and extracted any ounce of confidence. This was the picture I'd always imagined whenever an article said, "power couple." I couldn't tell what she was thinking, but I was too wrapped up in my own thoughts to care.

CHAPTER NINE

Hannah took yet another car from the infinite collection of her parents. I would've asked if her parents cared, but I assumed she would just say no. Or, she might've said that she didn't care if her parents cared. Even with my dad's blood running through my veins, Hannah kept me guessing. In all honesty, after all the conversations we'd had in the past few weeks, I may have not known her at all.

We jumped into what looked like lingering night parked inside a garage. Hannah claimed it was a car, but I didn't know that they made cars with so much darkness. When I relayed the thought to her, she didn't laugh. She only looked forward to her next destinations: the door, the seat, the road in front of her. She didn't say anything—at least, not with her mouth. Her eyes told me a different story. The only problem was that they each had a thousand tongues talking, each in a language I didn't speak.

Hannah didn't turn on the radio, and I had no idea how to myself. But I was desperate to break the silence. I grabbed my wallet from my back pocket. There was the business card from Melissa

Lund. I called the number on the card. "Melissa Lund, CNN, what can I do for you?" she greeted me in a very business-like tone.

"Ms. Lund, this is Tom," I answered.

"Tom!" she exclaimed in an odd sort of tone. It wasn't dread or excitement. I couldn't tell what it was. I waited for her to say more, but she failed to say any more words.

I began talking. "We need to speak with Daniel."

"No, Tom." Now, I could hear her tone. It was cautionary. "You have to leave," she said with the finality of a mother.

I was speechless for a few seconds. "What?" I asked in disbelief.

"Get out of here," she warned. Suddenly, she hung up. I stared at the phone and redialed the number. There was no response.

Hannah was too focused on destroying the air particles in front of the car to notice the conversation that took place beside her. She didn't look angry, but her driving made me believe differently. I didn't know if she even knew that I was on the phone.

"I called one of Daniel's cronies just now," I told her. She seemed to jump a little bit. I proceeded to tell her the whole story.

She was instantly suspicious. "Don't believe her," she said. "We are going to see Daniel." She stared straight ahead again and fell back into her odd, trance-like state.

"Right," I agreed, not wanting to look at her. I almost wished that I could open up her head underneath the platinum, soft hair. Thinking about it, I'm sure the pressure would be enough to shatter my skull; the way she drove with such intensity suggested that there was more going on in that mind than mine could imagine. I didn't know how she could bottle it all up like that, even if I didn't know what it was.

We arrived at the office in half the time it took a few days ago. She didn't take her eyes off the prize when she said, "Come on; let's go." She took some sunglasses from the car and slipped them on before stepping out of the car. I was a bit clumsier and slower, but, by the time we got to the door, her confidence rubbed off on me, and we were both marching to the door with power.

We walked in the door and I led her straight to the stairs. Neither of us missed a beat, knowing exactly what the other was thinking. This time, the silence was okay. We didn't need to speak to communicate. For what we needed now, we were the power couple. We looked the part, we acted the part, and we were the part.

We didn't hesitate when we reached the door and charged through. I knew what to expect, and I hoped my descriptions were enough for Hannah. When I looked at the scene, though, it wasn't at all what it was last time.

I paused and reevaluated the office. Everyone was bustling twice as fast and working three times as hard. However, there was about ten percent of the staff. I immediately attributed this to the earliness of the morning. I checked the clock. It was about six o'clock. It's not that early, I observed. I shook it off and took off, Hannah following without losing a step.

We strode quickly to Daniel's office and knocked on the door. His low, smug voice called out, "Yes, yes, come in."

We went into the room with louder steps and more purposeful faces. He didn't notice. He was on the phone and not looking. He was talking quickly and loudly, but I couldn't catch more than a few words. We continued to stare him down until he was done. I could only imagine how Hannah looked right now. With her shades on, she probably looked the part she had played. She looked powerful, ruthless, and ready for the kill. Even though I didn't break my gaze from Daniel, I knew that Hannah's face bore into Daniel's soul, extracting the essence of his terrible nature.

Finally, he disconnected and looked up. "Oh," he remarked, "you." His words held the intention of swatting me off like a fly, but I wouldn't budge. He showed the smallest sliver of surprise, but continued like it was more of an amusement. He nodded toward Hannah and said, "I see you've brought your vampire with you." He seemed to growl on the word, but his face said something different. It was like some kind of joke to him—pulling kids on a string and watching them get mad.

"This is Hannah," I said and took the chance to look at her. She looked perfect, exactly how I'd imagined. "We're here to know, what the hell?" I didn't flinch at the unprofessional language. It was called for.

He gave a one-syllable chuckle. "Which part are you talking about?" he asked. This was how he had his fun; he kept secrets and only told half-truths. I was beginning to understand how this man operated.

"The video," Hannah said coldly.

"Ah," he said, "the video. You are, of course, asking about the second one, right?" We nodded in response. It was a direct nod, obviously intended to shoot missiles in his direction. Unaffected, he continued, "That one had something that yours didn't. We've had it on file for a few weeks now."

We looked at him expectantly. He stood there smiling, relishing in the moment. He was really starting to piss me off. "Their video is real," he said.

It was just like in the movies with his last words. The world spun around quickly as he said the sentence in slow motion, resounding all around. The Earth focused all of its energy on that moment right there, stilling it to a silence.

"What?" I asked, trying to stay in skepticism. He was full of it; he had to be. My mind was sure of it. Yet, my body didn't agree. It began to tremble. I began to sweat as all of my confidence began to seep out my toes and onto the floor under my shoes.

He shrugged. "It's your choice as to whether you'd like to believe the truth or not. The rest of the country seems to," he replied. I couldn't tell whether he was bullshitting or not. The idea was absurd, impossible even, but something in me was starting to believe. That part of me started tremors in my heart, and made my legs grow weak.

Daniel turned on the television. I watched the new video in its entirety for the first time. It showed, at first, kids just having fun in the snow at night, obviously cold, with only a small fire to keep them warm. After that, I couldn't take the whole thing in. At some point, someone dropped the camera, and there was screaming. Something human, yet inhuman, tore through the forest. I watched again in horror as this real vampire destroyed these kids.

"R-real?" Hannah asked, not bothering with sentences.

"Yeah," Daniel responded, "and I've got a lot of work to do now. Bye." He waved us off.

I didn't move, not really knowing what happened. Without thinking about it, I asked, "Why did you need our video?"

Daniel seemed to slow down on his work, but he didn't respond. He was obviously interested. I kept on. "If you had a real video, why did you need ours?"

That made him stop. He looked up and

smiled a malicious smile. I stumbled backward a bit, almost afraid. "Thomas, my boy, we need ratings. You know that. That's what you pitched to your local news." I wondered how he knew that, but he was still talking, and I had too much curiosity to cut him off. "There were two things we needed to shoot our ratings through the roof." He paused. Whether it was to wait for me to ask, or it was for dramatic effect, I don't know. Regardless, I stayed quiet until he answered, "Theatrics and a poster boy.

"The theatrics provide something people want to watch—something that will keep their attention. With today's special effects and in-your-face blogs, the attention span is lower than ever. We needed sexy. We needed violent. We needed dirty."

I almost spat right there. He used us. He knew it was real and that everyone was in danger. He kept the information, trying to get the last bit of ratings to hit the ceiling. He was the dirty one there, not us.

"And, out of all of the videos, real or fake, yours was the only one that provided the final thing we needed to get the story along. We have someone to blame. Or, I guess, someone to hope for, if you get the right person. You, captured in full blood and dirt, are going to stick in the mind of everyone. They all know your name, and they all know who to go after for revenge, or who to turn to for help. But, you—you are the final piece,

Thomas. Now, get out of my office before they start beating down my door. I don't want to have to pay to get it replaced."

We left the office in silence. I couldn't begin to contend with what I'd just heard. I knew I did the world a favor. I pushed the truth into the front, even with a lie. How I felt was a different matter. I felt dirty and used. Without paying attention, I ran into someone.

"Tom!" she exclaimed. "Why haven't you left?" It was Melissa.

I couldn't speak. I couldn't process the mess that was my mind at that moment. She continued, "You are in terrible danger. You have to leave." She was holding onto my shoulders, gripping them with a strength I couldn't see. She rolled her eyes. She pulled a thick envelope from the stack of papers in her hands. "Here's your money. It's in cash. Now go." Before I could respond, she was pulled away by someone else talking in a hurried voice.

I stared as she was led off and down in another direction. I continued the empty stare, not fully processing what was in front of me. People were moving, working. I was just there, standing. Eventually, an ice cold realization flushed through my veins slowly, starting at the tips of my limbs until it reached my brain and my heart.

I was in danger. We were all in danger. I sucked in a deep breath, unsure of what to do.

Hannah pulled at my sleeve. Softly, she said, "Come on. Let's go." Her voice echoed in my head, but it never quite took hold. Nevertheless, I allowed her to pull me back to the stairs. When we shut the door, we were left alone with the concrete stairs. Every step we made was amplified by three-hundred percent. I suddenly became very tense, and my ears strained for any sound that didn't belong. Every few steps, I would stop and listen, imagining that I heard other steps above us. Whenever I stopped, the area was silent, except for the sound of our breathing.

Hannah always stopped when I did, not making a comment, or even a sound. I didn't look at her, but I knew that her confidence had faded with mine. I never noticed—until we had almost reached the bottom of the stairs—that she was still holding onto my arm.

I took one last listen at the foot of the stairs. I heard the click of a door upstairs. I froze, keeping my ears focused upwards. The steps that followed were light and quick, taking the stairs rapidly and closing the gap between us. My heart began racing, beating inside my ears. Even though I had no idea what the danger was—if there was any—, I still had the urge to run. Hannah's hand gripped my arm tightly, her nails digging into the fabric of the sleeve. Before the steps could reach the floor above us, we pushed through the door. My eyes darted around the room, looking for any danger that lurked in between us and the safety of Hannah's car.

The room was completely empty. I didn't take the time to look around when we arrived, and was shocked by the large, motionless room. No one waited on the sides. No one was at the desk. No one was bustling through the door. It was just as silent as the staircase, leaving me to tense my muscles more. I jerked my head around, beginning to sweat, waiting for something to jump out and attack.

I forgot about the steps behind us until the door opened. I jumped and spun around. At that moment, I felt like I was about to die. My body would be ripped into pieces, and my mind would cease to think. Behind us was only a woman in her late thirties. I didn't get a good look at her, for she barreled past us, taking her soft steps out the door at double the normal pace. I watched the door for a few seconds after she left, and then followed her lead with Hannah in tow.

We quickly made our way to Hannah's car. We had only been inside for ten or fifteen minutes, but life was changed forever. I still couldn't discern the possibility. It seemed all well when I was trying to convince the dim-witted masses, but when Daniel was convinced, there might be a problem. I may have hated him with every fiber of my being. He may have been a manipulative, conniving, dirty man. However, I knew he was intelligent.

Hannah and I sat in her car silently for a

moment. I continued to scan the area, looking for potential danger. To be perfectly honest, I had no idea what to look for. I knew it was there, though. It was waiting.

I looked over at Hannah. She was growing paler by the second.

"Let's get home," I suggested. She nodded in agreement and took off. Any driving she had on the way here was nothing compared to what it was then. She drove about twenty or thirty miles over the speed limit, diving around the occasional car.

We were at my house before I knew it. We didn't say a word on the entire ride there. Her car sat in idle as she waited in front of my yard. She continued her silence, but it was a different silence than before. Her eyes were wide and glossy, like she wasn't focused, or that she was about to cry. She gripped the wheel tightly, turning her knuckles white as snow.

I wanted to ask her if she was okay, or if she wanted to come in, or something comforting, but my own brain was muddled and tense with fear. I could only muster a good-bye. She wasn't much better. She nodded at me, and still said nothing. After waiting for her to say something—anything —I finally gave up and prepared to leave the car.

I put my hand on the cold handle and took my time. I looked around the area as much as I could, to prepare to face the danger. I took a long, deep breath, prolonging the last few seconds I had in the pseudo-safety of the car. When I opened the door, I was hit hard with a blast of cold air. I instantly cut through it, racing to my front door. I didn't take the time to look at my surroundings, fishing for my keys as I ran. It was a short distance, but it felt like I was in a mile-long sprint. Every second counted, and, while I didn't see it, it felt like I was being chased.

When I reached the white door, I scrambled through my keys, shaking. I tried to pull out the right one, but my shivering hand dropped them. I took the time to look behind me. The bustling wind was too loud for me to hear any oncoming danger, but my eyes scanned the area. I found nothing, but I could feel it creeping behind me. I could almost feel sharp nails digging into my shoulder, readying my neck to be intruded. I fumbled as quickly as I could, trying to get my keys back in my hand.

At last, I finally had a firm grasp on the correct key. I shoved it toward the lock, missing a few times. I probably dented both the lock and the key, but it didn't matter to me. When it slid into the lock, I turned it as hard as I could, making it more difficult to unlock the door. Eventually, I got it unlocked and burst through the door. I slammed the door behind me, locking it and putting on the deadbolt. I breathed heavily against the door.

I then set to work closing all of the curtains and blinds, checking outside first. I turned off all of the lights and stopped any unnecessary electronics. I was left in a dark, silent house. I hoped that it wouldn't set off any mental sensors, but I had no idea how to stay off the radar completely.

I saw that my dad fixed the window, so I felt it was safe to turn on the heat. It didn't make much noise, and, with the dropping temperatures, we'd need it to survive. When I thought about the drafty house, I thought about Alicia's house, and how we left Jack there. I quickly sent a text to Jack saying, "go home". I felt a vibration, probably him asking me why, but I was too numb to answer. I was surprised I even had the focus to send him the first text.

I collapsed on the couch in the dark and watched the news for hours on end, watching the murder count skyrocket. I didn't move for hours I couldn't even count. I kept the volume low, listening for anything out of the ordinary, but I could only hear the wind outside and the slight hum of the heat. I might've fallen asleep a few times, but it was a light, easily interrupted sleep. I was in the light sleep when I was jolted awake by someone trying to open the door. I heard the lock click and then the thump of the dead bolt.

"Tom?" I heard my dad call. I jumped up and unbolted it. I ushered him in swiftly and bolted it back up as soon as he stepped in. "Why is the deadbolt locked?" he asked. I didn't respond. I instantly turned around and hugged him and held him for the longest time I had since I was five. A lot of things I'd never been able to say went into that hug, but I knew there was a lot more that needed to be said. He hugged me back, but lightly.

"What happened?" he asked, concerned.

"Real." was all that came out of my mouth. I didn't know how to phrase the statement. Words like "vampire", "death", and "scared" flashed through my head, but they didn't create coherent sentences.

My dad gave me a very puzzled look. I took a deep breath, trying to make it coherent. "I think they're real," I said.

"What are?" he asked. He paused for a moment to think. "The vampires?"

I nodded.

He looked at me in a way that said he obviously didn't believe me. "Tom, Hannah isn't a vampire," he responded. "I think you need to lie down."

"Not Hannah!" I yelled in frustration. He didn't understand yet. I pointed at the television. "Look!"

He turned his head to the television. It was showing a highlight reel of my video again, mixed with commentary. "Isn't this what you wanted?" he asked. "Now the world believes that vampires are real. You can't buy your own con."

I fell silent. Is he right? I asked myself. Am I falling for my own trick? I shook it off. This wasn't my trick; this was someone else's truth. I'd been watching the news for hours. I knew. "You'll see." was all I said.

I walked off to my room and I waited. He didn't follow. I'm not sure what I was waiting for, but I was waiting. I sat on my bed in silence. I didn't go on the computer or turn on my own TV. There was nothing I could do. I brought a plague upon the world. What did I do?

I was left alone with my thoughts for a while until I drifted off into a black sleep. I awoke several hours later when it was still dark. I shuffled down back to the television. I saw my dad sitting on the couch. His eyes were locked onto the screen. His mouth opened in horror every few seconds. I turned over to see what he was staring at.

The headline said, "Minnesota Under Attack". It showed the massacre of many people here and there, all in places I know and places I'd been. Cars packed the highways, desperately trying to get away. I cringed as I saw a vampire thrust his arm through a window and pull out a screaming passenger. Right before the vampire bit her, the camera changed to another scene of terror. It kept flashing to different, terrible scenes of mass destruction. Now, my father believed me.

We sat in compete quiet, aside from the roaring sounds of the television. It was surreal. Vampires actually existed, and they were terrorizing the state we called home. These people fleeing and being killed were people we could have known, people we've bought groceries from or said hello to on the street. I tried not to look at the terrified faces; I didn't want to recognize any. At that point, I knew my dad made that very mistake. He had a sharp intake of breath and a tear welled up in the corner of his eye.

I turned off the television. My dad didn't move. He opened his mouth to speak, but nothing came out. I knew the feeling. There was so much to say, but there weren't any words for it.

Nothing was the same.

CHAPTER TEN

I walked over to the refrigerator and grabbed my dad another beer. He was never much of a drinker, but he always had some on hand for special occasions. This was quite an occasion. I held one in my hand for myself. He needed to steady himself, and I needed it just as much, if not more.

When I handed him the beer, he saw the extra one in my hand, but didn't give it a second thought. He would always understand. I cracked it open and began to drink it down. The cool sensation of the bitter liquid ran down my throat, and just the thought of what was coming relaxed me. My mind would soon be at ease. My dad's did not seem to rest. He began to steady his pace on his consumption. He watched me with a wary eye as I skillfully drank the liquid without as much as a flinch. If he wasn't tipsy, I probably could have earned a lecture.

"Rachel," he mumbled. It was the name of a girl that was shown killed. He once sold her a car. They weren't close. They'd only shared a few conversations and one lunch, but the reality of her death was devastating all the same. He began to silently cry. I knew that it was mostly the alcohol, but I couldn't help but feel him. It was the end of all we knew, and she was just the first.

He reentered his quick pace and drained the bottle within seconds. It was the end of the world, and he was going to drink himself stupid. He slammed the beer on the table, but it instantly tipped and fell to the floor. We both looked at it, but neither of us picked it up. He looked at me with teary, bloodshot eyes. There were dark circles touching on the bottoms of his sockets. It looked less as if he was up at two in the morning, and more like he hadn't slept for days. I grabbed his arm and said, "Come on, Dad. It's time for bed." I tried to pull him up, but he just stared at me in defeat.

I hoisted his arm over my shoulder and used all of my strength to pull him up. He was heavy, but he used a small bit of his own strength to keep himself up. I dragged him down the short hallway to his bedroom. I set him down on his bed, and he instantly curled up in it. I took a blanket and threw it over him. He clung onto it and closed his eyes. That was my cue to leave the room.

I shut the door gently and sat on the rough carpet. My back rested against his door, and I felt numb. What have I done? I asked myself. I couldn't stop thinking it. It was entirely my fault. I brought the destruction of the human race in my selfish quest for fame. But, there was nothing I could do. The damage was done, and I was powerless to help. All I could do was wait here. Wait for someone else to fight the battle; wait for the vampires to find me; wait to die.

That's when the hot liquid began to seep onto my face. I wasn't the crying type. Not that I was macho, but I never seemed to have reason to. Even if I couldn't quite fathom why, I was finally crying. I cried until the world faded back into the black of a dreamless sleep. When I woke a few hours later, it felt as if no time passed at all. My body still ached with exhaustion, and my mind continued exactly where it left off. The only difference wasn't in me at all; it was outside. The sun was up.

I never listened as a child to adults telling me not to look into the sun. Now seemed like a great time to thank myself for that. I stared into its beauty. It was a mark. It showed that I survived the night. It showed that there was hope. It showed that I was safe for a few meager hours. *The sun is my best friend.* That thought dragged me back to reality. Jack, my best friend, was in danger. I doubted that he even knew what was going on.

I searched frantically for my phone. Eventually, I found it on the floor of my bedroom. I scrolled through the mass of meaningless text messages from the other night. It hardly seemed that our harmless video had surfaced less than forty-eight hours ago. The only text from Jack said, "ok". It amazed me sometimes how he could have so much blind faith. He relied on others so much to do the thinking for him that it scared me to know what he'd do once he moved away—off to college or some job or even just out of his parents' house. If he stayed alive that long... I couldn't help thinking. I tried to shake it off, but it repeated in the darker edges of my mind, reminding me every thirty seconds that he might be dead.

"im coming over" I sent. I received no immediate response. I didn't exactly expect one. It was still in the early hours of the morning. He might have been up for school at this time, but it was the weekend. I stopped my thoughts. Was it the weekend? I pondered. I had been so preoccupied that I had no idea what day it was. The video surfaced on... I couldn't think of it. I tried to backtrack more. The interview was on Tuesday, I recalled. I remembered the secretary's voice telling me so. I tried to calculate the days since then, but I began to get dizzy. I shook it off. I had more important things to take care of. I needed to warn Jack.

I put on a coat and went outside. It wasn't much colder than yesterday, but I knew temperatures were going drop. A snowstorm was pointed our way—one of the few things the local news tried to slip in between reports of massacre. I looked at the blazing sun again and willed my eyes not to shut. In just a few days, we might be in danger, not only at night, but also during the day. I had no idea if a certain teen romance novel was right and vampires could go into cloudy weather unaffected.

I hurried to my car and started it up. I started driving the memorized way to Jack's house. He was only about two or three miles away, living in the same type of neighborhood I did. Houses were built twenty to thirty feet apart, only half had driveways, and children were always out front. It wasn't the same today, though. There weren't many cars parked on the streets. There were no kids playing outside, and everything was empty. The wind pushed on my car, and I battled it back.

I arrived at Jack's house and jumped out of my car without bothering to even shut the door. His mother answered. "Hi, Tom. Jack's sleeping, do you want me to—" She worked the night shift at a farm. I had no idea what she could've possibly have been doing at a farm at four in the morning, but she always got home at around seven. She must've just gotten home. Her hair was a bit dirty and still styled. She was obviously a working woman with a few bags under her eyes, a multitude of non expensive clothing, and simply painted nails. She had a nice expression on her face at all times, and it was complimented by her always kind demeanor. Her husband was away in India on business and always sent money, but sometimes, it just wasn't enough. They had five kids including Jack, and he wasn't exactly a breadwinner.

"No, that's okay. I'll get him," I hurriedly

interrupted. I ran past her. She would know soon enough. I already had to break the news to my own parent. I didn't want to have to do it for someone else's. I was a little intrigued to know why she didn't know yet. It was all over the television, and I wouldn't be surprised to hear of frantic phone calls made from all over the country.

I reached Jack's room. He was sprawled all over his tiny bed. The sheets were only half on and the blankets were discarded to the floor. I shook him awake. "Jack!" I exclaimed.

He mumbled something. He always was the heaviest sleeper I'd ever seen. I continued to shake him. "What?" he finally said.

"Jack," I said breathily, "the vampires, they're real."

He gave me a fake laugh. "Right. Why are you really here?"

"No!" I said. "That is why I'm here! They're fucking real."

His face turned a little more serious. "Dude, that's not funny," he stated.

I searched around his room. We'd grown so distant ever since the movie, that this room was now an uncharted forest. I looked around for a television. "Dude, where's the TV?" I asked.

"Downstairs," he replied sleepily.

I grabbed a fistful of his shirt and dragged him down the stairs. He wasn't helping me at all. When we arrived at the living room, I threw him onto the couch. He didn't make any comments.

He simply yawned and rubbed his eyes. Luckily, saving me the agony of trying to figure out someone else's television, his mother already had her eyes glued to the screen. She must have just started watching.

Jack's eyes bolted open when his mother finally started screaming. Before anything came from his open mouth, he looked at the screen and fell into a trance. His eyes glazed over and he watched the screen, as if it were just a normal movie. There was nothing real about it. He was dead wrong.

He shook his head and simply said, "No."

I fully faced him. "What do you mean, 'no'?" I remarked angrily.

"No," he said. "This isn't happening." It wasn't a frantic, head-shaking remark. It was like he truly thought it was still a joke.

"Jack!" his mother screamed. "It's right in front of you!"

"It's another trick," he assumed calmly. "If you guys are done, I'm going back to bed." He started to walk back towards the stairs. I stared at him open-mouthed.

"Jack!" He ignored me. How can he just ignore that this is happening? I asked myself. For as long as I'd known Jack, I never expected this from him. All that blind faith, when it mattered, disappeared. He faded up the steps as I stayed rooted to the spot, unsure of what to do. I looked at Jack's mother. She stared at the top of the steps with tears in her eyes. Behind her, I saw teeth sinking into the flesh of a squirming young woman.

I left Jack's house without words. I walked to my car slowly and stepped inside, but didn't pull out yet. I looked up at the sky. The sun was covered lightly by clouds. Goosebumps pulled themselves up on my skin at the insecurity. *Can the sun still stop them if I can't see it?* I questioned. I felt a chill as the wind began to whisper its way over. The storm was still a few days away, but I could feel it coming.

I made sure that every door was locked and began to breathe deeply. I turned on the radio, but all local stations were panic and could not speak of anything but the vampires. I shut it back off. I pushed my head back up and looked around. I didn't know where to go. Nothing was safe. My house could never hold off vampires. My car was not any better.

I shifted into reverse and drove out of Jack's driveway. I pushed the speed limits as I explored the too-familiar streets. I didn't notice on my way, but I saw boarded up windows. After seeing the strength the vampires showcased on the news, a few flimsy boards could never hold them back. However, I didn't have any better ideas. My speeds raced towards insanity as I increased them in the uncertainty. I didn't know whether the police would even be watching for stupid teenagers right now.

I quickly rounded a corner and narrowly avoided a parked car. I felt like I should slow my speed, but I stared at the speedometer as my foot was cemented in the same spot. I no longer had control. The road stretched before me, but, to me, it went nowhere.

I heard a scream. Instinctively, I turned my head. There was a struggle at a house coming up. I couldn't see it yet, but I knew it was the vampires. It had to be. I pushed on the gas a little more and cautiously looked at the scene as I quickly passed it. A girl, one I knew from school, was running. In the second I passed, she impossibly caught my eye. The terror I saw through the tears was enough to rival any horror movie ever made. It made my heart stop in its tracks and made my lungs feel like they were underwater.

Unbelievably, I made a rash decision and turned around. It was an out-of-body experience as I followed the road back to the very reality I'd been spending this whole time fleeing from. Before I knew it, I was driving straight into the girl's front yard. I didn't stop to think about how much I was destroying the grass underneath. I pried my eyes away from the scene around, keeping my eyes straight ahead, and tried not to guess whether the lumps were pieces of the house or pieces of a body. I saw her cornered for only a second before there was a thump on my car. The large body hitting my car created a giant crack across my windshield, decorated with a crimson liquid. I held back the squelching as I slammed on the brakes and unlocked the doors.

I screamed, "Get in!" I reprocessed everything in my head with quick, shallow breaths. I couldn't remember a conscious thought that told my body to destroy the girl's front yard. I didn't think that I ever made the decision to ram the vampire with my car. I took my hands off the wheel. They were pale and shaking.

The girl was in my backseat sobbing. Unintelligible words ran from her mouth through the hiccups.

I wanted to tell her that it would be okay, but my mouth couldn't open. I was frozen. The girl screamed again. I turned to her and followed her line of sight. Right outside my car was the completely halved familiar body. It was Lisa, from the party—I had no idea how long ago. It seemed like years, but it couldn't have been more than a few weeks. It was a terrifying sight. I almost was killed by that. I almost had sex with that.

I saw what the girl was screaming at. The halves of the body were still moving. They were struggling closer to each other. My breathing stopped as I watched in horror. My foot, of its own accord, let off the brake. The car began to slowly move, and I jolted back to my duty. I had to leave. I didn't save this girl for her to be massacred minutes later. I slammed on the gas. I swerved the wheel and tried not to feel satisfied or sick as there was a crunching of a skull under my front wheel. I decided not to look in my rear-view mirror until I was a safe distance away.

I didn't pick a destination; I just drove faster than I had in my life. I wanted to drive away from the horror, from the danger. I wanted to drive away from the whole world, but I was pretty sure the road didn't reach that far.

The girl cried herself into silence. It was eerie. Even if I didn't know what death smelled like, it hung in the air. It didn't help that the windshield wipers could only smear the liquid staining my front window. I couldn't see very well, but I didn't really care too much.

I stopped at a gas station. I parked next to a gas pump to use the windshield cleaners. As I wiped it off, chills ran up my arms, even if the blood seemed to radiate heat. I cleaned it three times, but it still stayed on the edges. I cleaned it another time, less gently. It was like I was trying to cleanse the whole world from the terror I'd inflicted upon it, but it wouldn't quite go away. It was stuck in plain view, just like the way the dark blood lay undisturbed in the middle of the windshield, right in the crack. There was nothing I could do. I'd already done the damage, and I'd have to live with it.

I finally gave up on having a clean windshield and walked into the station. As soon as the door chimed from opening, I saw disarray. No one was inside, and I guessed that the attendant left. I didn't see blood or bodies around, so I assumed the mess was from looters. The cash register was on the floor, surrounded by broken boxes of cigarettes. A few shelves were completely tipped over, spilled contents scattered the floor.

I waded through the mess to the fridge. The contents inside were lopsided and some threatened to fall out if you opened the door. However, all of the doors were intact. I opened the door, spilling some bottles on the floor. One was glass and shattered instantly, drenching my shoes in green tea. I didn't pay much attention to it; I simply pulled some drinks out. They were still cold.

With no one to pay, I almost didn't bother going to the counter, but I did, and took a look behind the counter warily. I almost expected something to jump out at me, but there was nothing there but spilled tobacco. I jumped over the counter and rummaged through the garbage to find the first intact cigarette box I could. I slipped it into my pocket.

I left the station, hearing the chime echo through an empty store. I arrived back at my car, the girl eying me carefully. I opened the door and sat in the driver's seat. I turned and handed her one of the drinks.

"Here," I said. She grabbed the drink and quickly scrambled up to the front seat. She grabbed my hand and simply looked at me with fearful eyes. She was acting like a lost six year old. It was the first time I'd gotten a good look at her.

She was small with short brown hair. I'd seen her before. She was a freshman at my high school. I thought that we may've even had a conversation at some point. In any other situation, I would have dropped her off somewhere, but she was in danger. We all were. I couldn't keep her with me forever, though. I didn't even remember her name.

Before I could say anything, she began to cry again. I didn't know what I would've said, anyway. Unsure, I put my arms lightly around her, and I let her cry for a little while longer. I couldn't do much else.

Soon, she settled back into her silence, and I backed out of the station.

Driving around, the girl eventually pointed to a house, and I entered the driveway. When she knocked on the door, another girl, also with short brown hair, answered and my girl broke down again. She was led inside, but I didn't follow. I walked silently back to my car.

I sat down in the seat, but didn't move. My hands gripped the wheel, but I was still in park. I had no idea where I should go. Eventually, I settled into past habits and set a course home.

CHAPTER ELEVEN

I returned to my house and everything was silent. Nothing seemed changed or destroyed. The world outside seemed entirely changed except for my own little square. Everything seemed normal here, even if what was outside it was broken.

I finally stepped out of my car and slowly walked to my house. I felt like I was breaking a certain vow or barrier when I stepped up the sidewalk. Everything was ominous and quiet. I could hear every footstep echoing to the sky.

I opened the door and said, "Dad?"

"Yeah, I'm here," he grunted. He sounded sluggish and slow. I came inside and chained the door, hearing the chain jingle as I let it go.

"Don't forget to chain the door," I said.

"Okay," he said lazily. I didn't know how long he'd been sitting there, in front of the television, but it was almost pathetic.

He was still watching. His eyes hadn't met mine when I'd walked in. I could feel a burning inside of me, longing to take back what I'd done, but I couldn't.

I sat down on a chair and watched the television with him, hoping beyond hope that they were going to announce that it was all a joke. I didn't care if people were going to start knocking down my door. I just wanted it to end. But I knew —I knew in the deepest part of me—that I'd seen it with my own eyes. That I'd destroyed it with my own car. But I still held on. I imagined that I'd look outside, and my car's windshield would be unbroken. I imagined that I'd simply wake up, in my bed, after a long night of working on the movie. I imagined that I never made the movie at all—that I was just daydreaming about getting famous, and I didn't have any skill at all. I imagined that everything was fine.

"Thomas Grant," a voice said and I jumped. At first I thought it was my dad, but he didn't have a woman's voice. I realized that I'd zoned out, and the news reporter said my name. I didn't hear what she said directly after that, but I recognized that she was about to show a clip. I got incredibly angry, ready to throw the nearest heavy thing at the screen. I never wanted to see my video again. They only played the last ten seconds, just enough to see my own face. I wanted to tear it off the screen, tear it off my own head and scream at it.

"This is all your fault! You killed hundreds of people!" I'd scream until my lungs burned out. I'd rip the skin into little pieces, irreparable damage to the cause of the irreparable damage of the world.

"...survivor and hero," the reporter said. I locked my eyes to the screen. They cut to another clip, with much lesser quality. It must've been from a webcam or incredibly old camera from a neighboring house. I saw a figure running and another one closing the gap in a second. Then, even through the horrible quality, I saw my car speed up and ram into the faster figure, cutting it disgustingly in half. I felt the bile build in my stomach, warning me that it was about to make a special appearance.

"Jenna Leers, 14, was saved by Grant this morning. Gregory Nichols, an adjoining neighbor, was capturing an attack on his webcam when Grant's car appeared..." She continued telling the story, but I already knew it. I was there.

"Tom?" my dad asked. He didn't say anything else, but his tone held concern, and just a bit of anger.

I didn't meet his eyes. I didn't know what to say, but I opened my mouth, hoping my nature would allow words to flow out. "I'm famous," I said, echoing Daniel's words. After that, the words really did begin to flow out of my mouth. "Daniel used me. He wanted me to be a poster child for all this bullshit. Now that this is here, people will be here any minute, waiting for me to be their savior. Everyone will know my name. Everyone will know where I am."

I took my hands to my temples, rubbing

them, wishing the whole situation would go away.

My dad was silent. When I calmed down, I looked at him, and he just looked straight ahead, with calculating eyes. Eventually, he stood up and began to shuffle through paperwork on the table.

"What are you doing?" I asked him. He couldn't possibly have the need for paperwork now.

He didn't look up from his work. "Getting ready for work tomorrow," he said matter-of-factly. My mouth dropped open.

It took me a moment to form words. I eventually said, "Work?" He grunted in agreement. "Even though the world is being attacked by vampires?" I pressed.

"What about them?" he asked seamlessly. I didn't know what changed in him. Every adult portrayed as an oblivious bastard on cartoons was portrayed perfectly on my dad at that second.

"You can't just 'go to work'! You could die!" I pleaded. He couldn't comprehend the blood that still filled in the crack in my windshield or the tears that dried up my backseat. My heart beat rapidly, even thinking about the encounter.

"We can die every day," he stated plainly. My mouth dropped open. I was about to become the one in denial. It was hard for me to believe that he said that.

I had no response. "But, you, and the..." I stuttered. My shouts clambered at the back of my throat; they didn't have any words.

He sighed and walked over to me. "Tom, one day, when you're older, you'll understand that you have to take risks in life. You have to stop living in fear," he explained. The words were like poison in my ears. They had no nutritional value, and they would get me killed.

The scene in the girl's yard replayed in my head. "I saw one!" I blurted out.

My dad, unbelievably, stayed calm. "Yeah, I saw a ton on TV, too—"

"Not on TV!" I interrupted. My blood began to boil. It was like trying to convince a brick wall to fly. "I saw a real one! I hit it with my car!" I shouted.

"I know," he said. "I saw it. Is it dead?"

I didn't expect him to ask that. "I don't know! Yes, no…" I impatiently answered. The tainted oxygen in my lungs told me differently. The lead weight inside told me that I did know. I know that Lisa wasn't dead. It was a horror movie, and the monsters always came back.

"Well, did you check?" he asked as if it were obvious.

"No," I responded, "but I saw it trying to…" I wasn't sure how to put it into words, but I made an awkward conjoining gesture with my hands and hoped it was sufficient for him. At this point, I didn't think that anything would be good enough. He'd built a wall around his consciousness and no amount of proof or data could penetrate it.

"Did you damage the car?" I almost lost it

when he said that. It was absolutely ridiculous. I was surprised that I didn't leave the room right then.

I felt the hot blood rush to my cheeks in frustration. "What do you mean, 'Did I damage the car'? Of course I did!"

"I'm not going to pay for that," he remarked.

That was when I threw in the towel. I stormed to my bedroom and slammed the door. I didn't know what to do. My life, my friends 'lives, and even my dad's life were all in complete peril. Everything I knew turned itself over. I panted in exhaustion and sat on my bed to gather my thoughts.

"Tom," he said on the other side of the door. I didn't answer. It was childish, but he was being just as immature, if not more. "Can I come in?" he asked, but I allowed my silence to carry on.

He let himself in and sat in my computer chair. "Tom, you can't expect me to pay—"

"It's not about the car!" I exclaimed. "You don't get it! We're going to die!" I didn't mean to put it like that, but I didn't take back the words. Although I didn't want to leave, and I didn't feel like I should, I knew that I had to. Even if I felt safe, I knew I wasn't. And, if my dad didn't stay safe, I'd never be safe.

"Tom," he said. "You're the poster child. You can't run away. People look at you now for hope, for guidance. You can't tell them to run away. You have to be here to tell them that they can live their lives; that they can go home."

"But they can't!"

"Yes, they can," he explained.   "You've shown them that they can fight.   Not just for themselves, but for everybody.   You have to be here, to lead them."

"I can't lead the world," I said.

"Yes, you can."

I didn't say anything after that.   He continued, "No matter where we go, people will know where we are.   People know your name, and people will know your face. It's better for everyone if we stay here."

I stared at him, without saying a word. Eventually, he simply got up and left.   I didn't move.   I stayed in my bed, trying to calculate my next move.   This stupid house, regardless of how secure I felt simply being home, was dangerous.   Where was safe? I asked myself.   I strolled to my computer and looked up "vampire attacks".   The search page was littered with blogs and videos.   There was also an immense amount of news articles.   I narrowed my search to those and skimmed through the first few pages of articles.   At the moment, the attacks seemed to be saturated in the Midwest—specifically Minnesota. There was a map of severity of violence, just like a weather map.   It grew like a disease, the point of conception, in a deep, dark burgundy, was my little town, seeming to point directly at my home.

The other pictures were cold and bloody,

and I tore my eyes away. The horror was unbearable. We had to leave. I didn't care what my dad said. We were leaving. I grabbed a suitcase and packed anything I might miss. As much as I wanted to feel like I could come back, I probably wasn't going to. I tried to pack away all of the little trinkets that had significant value to me, being careful not to miss any.

My hands arrived at the last birthday present my mother ever sent. It was a nicely decorated pocket knife. Thoughts began to tease themselves in my head. Running my hand along the handle, I remembered opening the small brown box with my name on it. I was young, not sure of my age. The box didn't come on my birthday. It was about four months after, but I didn't care. I knew she didn't forget. I recalled opening it and marveling at how shiny it was. I couldn't open it myself at the time, but my dad showed me how.

Originally, my dad took it right after showing me how to open it. I cried for hours. Eventually, he at least put it somewhere I could look at it, but it was too high for me to reach it. I would look at it every day and would imagine that my mom was there, giving it to me on my birthday. Sometimes, I would forget that she wasn't there, and would cry when I realized I imagined her up.

At some point, I stopped looking at it because it would make me cry with just a glance. Many years later, when I'd forgotten about it, I saw it from the corner of my eye. I was just tall enough to reach it, so I took it to my room. I didn't open it, but I put it on my desk, so I could hold it. I cried one last time that night. Afterwards, I never cried about her again.

I held it in my hands for a moment. It didn't just look good, but it was sharp and comfortable in my hands. My first instinct was to pack it, in order to save a memory of her. The second was a flashing bit of rebellion I undoubtedly inherited from her. I wanted to leave it to show I didn't care, but that thought left quickly.

No matter where we go, people will know where we are, my dad's voice echoed in my head. I opened the knife and looked at my reflection in the unscratched, clean surface. My face looked the same as it did in the video, maybe a bit cleaner, but mostly the same. I could almost see my name printed on my forehead, branding me for who I was. No matter where I go, she'll know where I am.

I decided that I'd keep the knife. As dirty as I'd been taught to feel about killing and violence, it felt right to have the thought of protection in my hands. All of the thoughts of the absent safety instantly secured themselves behind lock and key when I held it in my palms. I felt control.

I finished packing up everything else but left the knife in plain sight. When I finished, it was night again, and I heard my dad shut his door for bed. I pulled up a bag I'd found while packing. It opened easily, it was small, and it was light. I almost put the knife in first, but I wanted easy access to it. I decided instead to put it in my pocket. I practiced pulling it in and out. It was perfect. When I put it back in, I left a small bit of it poking out, imagining that my mother would come running to wherever it was, see the knife, and, well, I didn't know after that. She might cry, knowing that I never forgot about her all these years, and we'd hug and catch up.

I began to rummage the house for anything else I wanted on hand for emergencies. The first thing was a flashlight. I doubted that it could kill a vampire when the sun couldn't when covered by clouds, but it couldn't hurt. Next, I found some hand sanitizer, water bottles, and a few other first aid items. I added a few snacks from the kitchen along with candles and matches.

My hand lingered over the silverware drawer. I had my knife safely in my pocket, but I never knew what was going to happen, and I might need more. I tried to pull it open, but it was stuck. Right at that point, I was almost glad to be leaving this place. It was a piece of shit. Everyone I knew, which admittedly wasn't very many, had a nicer place than I did.

I pulled off my bag and pried at the drawer with both hands. Eventually, it became unstuck and flew out of its place. The silverware clamored around me, and I flinched. I looked instantly at the hallway and waited for the sound of an opening bedroom door. Holding my breath, I listened as closely as I could.

It never came. I breathed a sigh of relief and picked up the silver around me. I threw a few knives into the sack and tested the weight. It was beginning to get heavy. I knew that if I wanted to carry it around, I had to keep it as light as possible.

I tried to fit the drawer back into its spot, but I couldn't see with just the flashlight. I tentatively turned on the kitchen light and went back to the area. I still couldn't see it, so I reached my hand inside and felt around, hoping it wasn't a knife caught in there. At some point, my hand hit cold metal. Feeling it up and down, I immediately recognized it, even though I'd never held one before.

I carefully pulled the gun out. It was incredibly heavy in my hands. I stared at it like it was an odd sort of bug. As powerful as this protection may have been, it didn't feel the same as the pocketknife in my hands; it felt all wrong. I was afraid that I could set it off with the slightest touch. I set the gun on the counter, away from where I was putting the drawer back, and continued working.

When I finished, I approached the gun cautiously. I picked it up and imagined the added weight to my bag. I also imagined trying to take it out if I needed it. It would probably fall underneath some items. I could see myself trying to pull it out of the bag and the trigger catching on one of the knives, setting it off. I couldn't even bring up the thought of shooting it, even if it would save my life.

I slung the bag onto my shoulder, and carefully picked up the gun. I held it loosely and took it to my room. I set in on my desk and covered it with a shirt. I didn't want it, but, somehow, I knew that I needed it. I couldn't stand to look at it, though.

I turned off the lights and got into my bed. I slept lightly, listening on edge. I woke up constantly, and replayed the plan through my head again and again. I didn't know if it would work, but I prayed it would.

I tried to keep my thoughts on sleep, but my short dreams became confusing—full of vampires, many voices of my father, and an endless, bloody road.

I shot out of bed at the first light of the morning, even though I never set my alarm. I was on a mission. I hid my suitcase and bolted out of the house while my dad was in the bathroom. I was sure to make enough noise for him to know that I left. I got into my car and emptied my hands. I put the pack into the passenger's seat and looked at the gun. The passenger's seat looked too dangerous and suspicious at the same time. I looked around uneasily and put it into the glove compartment.

I started my car and drove off noisily. I smiled in satisfaction as my plan worked perfectly. I drove around the block and parked around the corner. My car was completely invisible on my dad's trek to work. The original plan was to get out of my car, taking my pack with me and watching the house in secrecy, but as soon as I opened the door, the cold wind hit me, bringing a chill under my skin. It wasn't just from the cold, but from what I knew the outside had. I could almost hear footsteps, malicious footsteps, carrying on the gusts and decided to stay in my locked car.

It took a while, but I watched as my dad finally left and drove away from our house. I locked my doors and ran to the house, trying to ignore the speaking wind, not seeing the sense in driving the short distance. It was a little cold, but it was bearable.

I had my keys ready to go before I left the car. I walked into my house and shot for my dad's room. I packed up clothes of his and looked around. I realized that I didn't know what my dad valued. I had to guess. For as close as I had thought we may have been, I really didn't know much about him at all. I hoped that the long trek to wherever we were going would bring us together.

Around his room, I saw a few things. I saw his high school diploma alongside his college degree. I saw trophies from back in his day, when he played football. I touched one and my fingers came back dusty. He didn't take care of them. They were in the back behind picture frames and knick-knacks, and he probably didn't even look at them. I assumed that he wouldn't miss them. I grabbed at the picture frames. Most of them were pictures of him with me, and I wasn't surprised. There was one picture that held a younger version of him with a small, paint-splattered woman in his arms. It was my mother. I covered it up and packed it away. I saw another picture. My dad was even younger. He must have recently left high school. He stood with another handsome young man his age. I've never seen this man before, and I can't recall my father talking of any friends from high school in-depth. The picture, however, was clean, but it was bent from over-handling. I packed that as well.

My hand fell over a stray sock, and I realized that I'd forgotten to pack those for him and myself. I cursed softly. Considering that I was already in his room, I packed his first. I opened up the sock drawer and found not only white socks, but papers. I took them out and they were mostly bank statements. I assumed that they were normal financial tracking, but, upon closer inspection, the numbers were wrong. The balance was always rising. It never fell from bills or expenses. The only thing inside was deposits. I stared at it, asking it for answers, but paper couldn't talk. I scanned it up and down, looking for anomalies, but found none until my eyes caught the owner of the account. At the top, it said, "Thomas Grant". This was my money.

I grabbed a few of the latest statements and shoved them into my pockets to deal with later.

I packed away some socks and searched his room for a bag like mine to carry essentials. I found one, slightly heavier, but I knew it would work. I packed it with water bottles and candles. As for weapons, I'd kept all of the good ones for myself. I made sure to grab some kitchen knives for him. Even with the heavier material, his pack seemed much lighter than mine. I almost felt bad, but I realized that I wasn't going to be leaving him. Besides, he had easier access to my pack than I did when I was wearing it. I tried to trick myself into feeling bad for myself, knowing that he had it better, but I knew it wasn't true.

I took one last sweep of the house to find anything we might want to come back for, but found nothing. I saw the television, but I could never bring that with. Without the television, the movies would be pointless as well. I looked at the beds and the blankets and the plates, and my heart felt heavy looking at how much we were going to leave behind. It felt as if I was leaving a whole life behind in this tiny house.

Suddenly, I heard a rustling, just outside the door. I spun around, but through solid wood. I grabbed the knife from my pocket and held it out in front of me. It was still pristinely clean, and I could see my own reflection in it. My eyes were dilated from fear, but the lids looked heavy with exhaustion. With the sporadic sleeping, I'd never given a thought to exactly how much I'd gotten. Or, in this case, how much I hadn't gotten.

I heard my heart beating in the dark caverns in my ears. I began to shake as my vision blurred. Instantly, I knew. They were here. They were coming to get me. My breathing became rugged. It hurt to inhale. "Be ready," I said aloud. Talking to myself was the only thing keeping my sanity tethered to my consciousness. At any other time, that may have been paradoxical, but I didn't care at that point. I continued, "You're the one who revealed them. They have no reason to hate you. You gave them freedom." I tried to betray myself into believing those words, but I knew I couldn't.

I was frozen in place, eager to look around. *Would they sneak up behind me? Pounce from the window? Would I even know?* I pondered. After waiting several agonizing minutes in silence, I exhaled. I hadn't known that my breath was held. I slowly shuffled to the window. I heard more rustling. I slowly moved part of the covering and peered out. My heart was pumping faster and faster as I looked into the eerie emptiness. I looked out toward the doorway.

There was nothing. I heard the breeze coming in through the cracks, but nothing more. Wary, I gathered everything up and quickly motioned to leave. Nothing stopped me except myself. There was no more rustling. It was only silence. Dead silence. I cautioned at the door as I opened it. I peered around. Nothing changed. I sprinted back to my car, not looking behind me. As I got in and locked the doors, I cursed myself. I couldn't believe what possessed me to leave my car there.

I locked the doors and started the engine. My sides were hurting as I was panting. I continued to look around nervously. There was still nothing. There were no kids, no cars, no one moving in the windows. I rapidly moved my car. I needed to get out. I couldn't help but continue to look from side to side. I felt them all around me. I swore that I could feel the cold breath on the back of my neck. I quickly turned around. There was nothing. I took the time to exhale deeply before turning back to the road.

There was, of course, something in front of me when I turned around. I'd drifted off the road, and was now headed for a tree. I slammed on the brakes. I stopped to breathe. Everything was happening at once. I was just kid; I couldn't handle this. I turned around to back up into the road. Everything in my backseat had jumbled around, opened, or created a mess. I let out a groan and tried to ignore it as I drove back onto the road.

I hadn't been to my dad's work in years. I never had a reason to. Living in a small town, I passed by it occasionally, but the route felt like driving into open water. Everything was quiet; I never saw anyone. Cars were missing, houses seemed empty, and there was no traffic. I couldn't even begin to deceive myself that it was normal. It wasn't. Nothing was normal.

I watched the clock as I drove. Every time

a minute passed by, my heart started pumping a little faster; it was a minute closer to nightfall; it was a minute longer I was in danger. I kept reading the street signs; they looked as though it was a foreign language I just learned. I understood the words, but it felt strange and unfamiliar. When I passed by one, I made a rash decision and took a right. It was Jack's street, and I had to know that he was okay. It was definitely out of my way. I never even knew that his street passed the way, but I knew which way to go.

I arrived and saw his family carrying boxes into a van. They were leaving, just as I was. I drove up and got out of the car cautiously. They were working incredibly quickly. They noticed me, but all I got were a few short hellos. When Jack came out carrying a particularly heavy box, he put it in and turned around to talk to me.

"Hey," he said. We shuffled around for a moment in awkward silence.

"Leaving, huh?" I asked, even if the answer was obvious.

"Yeah," he answered and paused. "You were right." He chuckled the most awkward chuckle that ever passed through his lips.

I sheepishly smiled. "I know." We held another silence. "So, where are you going?"

"Florida," he replied. "The attacks are all in the Midwest for now, so we're gonna go far. My dad's coming down, so we'll meet him there." The shuffling continued.

"So, I guess this is goodbye," I stated, trying not to let my voice betray me. There was a lead weight in my lungs, making it hard to get the words out without wavering. He had been my best friend for a while. Although he was a bit rude, a bit daft, and just a bit self-centered, I'd grown accustomed to it. I liked it.

He paused again. "I guess so." He didn't look at me. "We'll still have Facebook 'n stuff," he quickly added.

"Yeah," I agreed. "It's like you won't even be gone," I lied.

"Mmhmm."

The silence that held over the entire conversation took hold as we stood there. Neither of us was willing to convey what we were feeling, but it was there in front of our faces. I didn't need my dad's genes to tell me that he felt pretty much the same way I did.

"Okay, Jack, we're leaving, now," Jack's mother interrupted. The rest of his family got in the car, but Jack waited.

"Alright, well, goodbye," he said uncomfortably. He held out for a handshake. I took it. It didn't feel like a goodbye. It felt like closing a business deal. I almost wanted to hug him, but neither of us were the hugging type. We were men, and men didn't do that.

I simply got back into my car and took off. In my rear-view mirror, I watched them leave. My eyes stung, but I didn't cry. I was done crying a long time ago.

I kept driving, and it took me a moment to remember where I was going. Every stationary, silent thing passing me by looked even more foreign and strange than it did before. Without Jack, my best friend, nothing was right. He was one of the only things that made this city feel like home. Little by little, my city was drifting off the edge of the world.

It was a blur until I arrived at the dealership. It looked exactly as I recalled it, but even then, everything was unfamiliar. I remembered a gigantic grey building covered in large windows, but everything was smaller. Instead of hopeful couples and new families waiting to sign the papers, I only saw a dimly lit open space with one person staring out the window, refusing to look at the car that crowded his driveway every morning.

I pulled into the parking lot, right next to my dad, not caring about whether I was actually in a parking spot or not. No one was going to come in. I looked around in the maze of cars. It was so empty. The cars seemed so old and in disrepair, even though some of them were only a year or two old.

I scanned the lot, hoping for even one person, but there was no one. As a kid, when I was here, there were always a few lookers at any given time. Now, there were none. Just like the rest of the city, a morbid silence fell over everything.

I walked to the building and through the

doors nonchalantly. "Hey," I greeted.

He didn't turn from the window. "Hi," he replied.

I took a deep breath. "We're leaving," I told him, trying to make it sound like it was no big deal.

"No we're not," he retorted, still not taking his sight from the window, sounding equally unaffected.

"Yes," I argued, "we are. I've packed your stuff." I became a bit more forceful.

"Put it back because I'm not going," he responded.

"Dad," I pleaded, "we have to."

He put a hand on the window before he turned to face me. His eyes were lost and empty with dark circles underneath. It looked as though he'd aged five years in the past few hours. The eyelids were drooping and every blink lasted a second more than it needed to.

"I-I can't," he stuttered.

I was confused. "Why?" I asked him.

He looked back sadly at the window for a moment. "I grew up here. Everything I know is here," he admitted.

I looked at him. A tear slowly fell from his eye, and he turned back to the window. I hugged him. It was awkward and odd, but it was good. His breathing was deep and staggered.

I let go, and he sat down in a chair at his desk. I sat in a chair opposite him. He wiped away a few tears. "I was born here," he explained. "My parents lived in the same house we do. I remember waking up in the morning, and my mom was always in the kitchen with breakfast. Except Saturdays—my dad always cooked breakfast on Saturdays. Bacon and eggs every week. That was always my favorite. Some mornings, I can still smell them cooking." He took in a breath like he was going to cry, but didn't.

He pressed on, "I remember going to the same elementary school you did. Back then, there was only one school for the little ones. But, back then, we didn't have so many people. I met my best friend Dave back then. He lived up on 42nd Street—the blue house. I went there almost every day until I was seventeen. I remember asking him why his house was blue, while all the others were white, but he didn't know. The family was always a little different, but I liked it. My family was conservative and traditional. ' How a family should be, 'my dad always said.

"Dave was always the weird kid at school. I was popular—football, parties, and everything else. No one liked Dave, though, and I couldn't figure out why. When I was seventeen, I stopped trying to bring him into my circle. Not that I didn't like him, but I simply gave up. I started trying to hang out with his group, including his other best friend, Mary." A little alarm went off in my head. "Yes, that was your mother.

"At first, she was the weird artist girl who quoted poets no one ever heard of. I began to hang out more and more with her, and I realized that it ran deeper. She was artistic in her heart. She had these dreams for life—ones I could never imagine. I looked at my own parents, and I looked at her, and I realized that I wanted the life in her head, and not the one in my parents'. I asked her out, and, of course, she instantly said yes.

"For the longest time, things came easy. It was perfect; my best friend and my girlfriend were always together, so it was always the three of us. One day, Mary let a little secret slip. Dave was gay. I didn't think anything of it. Sure, I'd slept at his house, but he never tried anything. When I told my parents, they weren't okay. They told me never to talk to him again, and they forced me to go to church on Wednesdays as well as Sundays. I told them to screw off, but they didn't like that either. They attributed that to my rebel girlfriend and the abomination. One day, they told me to pack my things up and we moved out of the state.

"I couldn't call my friends or Mary, so I had to break it off. We exchanged addresses, but the letters lasted for only a few weeks. I always wished that I could've stood up to my parents and stayed. I never saw anything wrong with my friends, but I began to see the wrong in my parents. I drifted further and further from them. They eventually stopped making breakfast for me in the morning. When I was nineteen and stupid, I moved back here. I knew that I was going to struggle with money, but this was where I needed to be."

He took in another deep breath. "When I came back, Dave was gone. But Mary was still there. We got together, and the sparks went off again. From that point on, I told myself that I would support Mary in everything, regardless. We eventually moved into my old house, got married, and had a kid. I watched that kid grow up on the same steps I did. I never left because a part of me will always be in that house, and a part of me will always wait for Dave to come back for me to apologize." That's when more tears began to fall down his cheeks. He rubbed his sleeve against his eyes.

I never saw this side of my dad. I never knew him to have friends. I said, "I'm sorry." I knew it wasn't enough, but it was something.

Through his sleeve, my dad said, "I'm a stupid, selfish old man. I'm sorry. I shouldn't keep you here. You're right. You're in danger. I just don't want to be alone. You can go. Leave me behind. I just can't leave. There's too much here. When you said that everyone knew you and would know you're here, I hoped that would mean Dave would come back, and know that I came back for him."

I sat in silent contemplation for a moment. It was dangerous, but it was going to be dangerous everywhere else, right? "I'm not leaving without you, Dad," I told him.

"No, no…" he mumbled as he shook his head.

"So, I guess I'm staying here," I declared. After everything I'd felt in this unsafe, burgundy city, it was the first decision I felt firm in, even if I made it in ten seconds. My dad was the most important person in the world to me, and I couldn't let him be alone.

My dad instantly got up pulled me into a hug—a real, awkward hug. He began crying again. He said, "Thank you" through the tears. After we broke, we sat there in silence. I couldn't go home. I would feel like a sitting duck. They were all around. Even if the weather didn't seem bad now, the snowstorm was coming. Any chance for sun was about to be destroyed.

So, I decided to wait there. At first, my dad pulled out a deck of cards, and we played for a good hour or so, but it got old. We tried talking, playing tic-tac-toe, and throwing a tennis ball—careful not to break a window—, but we couldn't do anything for too long. It was like we were just waiting for something to happen, even if we didn't want it to.

No matter what we did, I was always getting up for something. Sometimes, I would get water. Sometimes, I wanted to look out the windows. I couldn't stay in one place. I needed to stay active to stay alive, or so I thought.

I couldn't help but dwell on the immense space in this building. With just my dad and me, there was nothing to cover the quiet. Every day since the video, there always seemed to be this dead quiet that followed me around. It was like a cloud that shuttered my every conversation. They were incredibly comparable to the ominous clouds outside. I knew the storm was still a few days away, but every time a cloud would pass over the sun, our only hope, the world seemed to stop turning. I would hold my breath and expect my death to come crashing through the large, exposing windows, unannounced. *That's impossible*, I kept trying to tell myself. The windows could see everything. I would definitely see my demise before it came. That comforted me a little. I wasn't sure why; I knew it shouldn't.

During that entire day, I only saw one car passing by. It was strange to think that the whole town was suddenly gone. My entire life I had always seen people around and never thought anything of it. Now Jack was gone. Everyone was gone. I doubted that anyone even went to school. I thought of my classes, and how, oddly enough, I would miss them. I would miss listening to people talk about the latest gossip. I would miss my old lunch table. I would miss Hannah. She was probably on the first plane south. Her family was probably soaking it up on a sunlit cruise. I would miss Alicia and her cold demeanor. I even thought of our make out session and how I would miss that.

Lost in my silent, depressing thoughts, I nearly missed that it was almost sundown. My fingers began to tremble. I was going to die tonight, I knew it.

Thankfully, I was mistaken. My dad and I took turns sleeping and keeping watch. It was awful. I just stared out into the darkness, looking for any sign of movement. Luckily, being around heavy mechanical inanimate objects, it was easy to spot movement. Unluckily, any movement looked like the end. My dad and I both shared a fair amount of scares. It always went the same way. We shook the other awake and pointed. Then, we'd stare in fear until we found out it was a chipmunk or a leaf.

Every time I tried to sleep, it was hard to get to sleep without a thousand thoughts trying to take hold. During my last sleeping shift, I thought about my father. How he was waiting for Dave. He wasn't waiting for my mother, like I was. I knew that somewhere, he wanted her back, but not like I did. I took the knife out of my pocket and held it tightly in my hand, imagining that it was my mother's hand I was holding so tightly. I pretended that she was stroking my hair and whispering me to sleep.

I woke up to the sun and instantly shot up, looking around, scared. This will be our life, I stated to myself. I would wake up in a panic every hour or so. A pocket knife would be glued to my hand, and I was simply waiting for my death. Every hour it seemed, something depressing would sink in. But with the silence all around, it was natural for the human mind to find something to occupy itself. Then, my mind—and my body—found something else to focus on.

"Dad," I said, feeling like a child again, "I'm hungry."

He sat up straight. "I already ate all the food here. We'll have to go find some."

"Where?" I asked.

He looked at me as if I were insane. "The store?" he answered. "Just because we're attacked, doesn't mean we've been transported to some third world country."

I felt a little stupid, but, to be fair, I felt as though we were somewhere else. It was like I was on a side of unbreakable glass. I could see everything I knew, but it felt unattainable. We didn't get up for a while. And, although what he said made sense logically, I knew that he felt the same way I did. The world was different. The store was a mere mile or two away, but it could have been across the state for all it mattered. It felt like it wasn't close enough.

My father stood up, and I reluctantly followed suit. He took a set of keys, from a hook by his desk, which were obviously not his. We got to the door, and waited for a moment. I wasn't sure what we expected to happen in the few silent seconds, and I'm sure my dad felt the same, but there wasn't anything. I took a deep breath and opened the door. There was a bitter wind that bit at my skin instantly. My dad pushed in front of me and made it to a large, black SUV as quick as he could. I raced to follow and sat in the front seat.

We locked the doors quickly, and he started the car and rolled down the window a bit. He fumbled in his pockets and pulled out a pack of cigarettes. I watched him in fascination. I knew he smoked; there were secret signs everywhere. However, he had never done it in front of me, as far as I could remember. He lit it up and took a drag with a look of relief. The smell brought back memories of parties and secrets.

Tentatively, I asked, "Can I have one?" He looked at me for a second, a mix of shock and disappointment. Regardless, he sighed and handed me one and the lighter. The pack in my pocket felt a lot lighter as he handed me the cigarette. I knew I had some of my own, but giving one of his own to me was a sign that he'd be okay. Before I lit up, he started racing the car out of the lot. I touched the flame to the end and more memories came back—good and bad. In the end, all of them were hurting to remember. I knew I would never go to parties again.

I took a hit of the tobacco and waited a moment to feel the first high. The calming effect was instantaneous. I marveled at the tobacco's ability to slightly downplay the situation at hand. But it didn't last long. The world was more dangerous than I'd previously perceived.

Every mile was a lifetime, even though my dad destroyed the speed limits. When we finally reached the store, the sight was shocking. Every line in the parking lot was disregarded. My dad took no care to break the cycle and placed the SUV in a random spot. I threw open the door and ran. Behind me, I heard my dad with the same idea. I didn't stop until I stepped into the store and heard the doors close behind me. I doubled over and took quite a few long breaths. When I stood straight up, I looked around.

The scene first reminded me of the gas station, but worse. The store was completely trashed. Things were pulled off the shelves, broken. Nothing was stacked or orderly, and the shelves were scarcely stocked. The worst parts, to my horror, were the human remains. There were two or three scattered corpses, or so I assumed, but I didn't dwell on them. There was blood everywhere. There were stains from obvious struggles as well as from free-flowing wounds creating puddles. My stomach turned violently, and I was surprised that I wasn't currently heaving.

I turned around to see my dad assessing the situation. If he felt the same way, he didn't show it. But his words may have betrayed him a bit. "Let's get our things and get out as soon as possible." I nodded as he pressed forward, stepping over the debris like it was normal garbage.

I went around a bit slower, scooting around anything without letting my gaze linger on it. I had nothing in mind I wanted. I simply looked around the aisles quickly to find one with minimal damage. I passed a certain aisle with the most damage and could smell the strong odor of alcohol. On a cursory glance, I noticed that there was no alcohol left on the shelves. I supposed it made sense. I almost wanted a bottle of tequila myself. I quickly moved on, being absolutely sure that I didn't look at the floor.

I found my way to the frozen food section. It seemed pretty intact. After walking down, I learned that the mess was behind the doors, just like at the gas station. However, I didn't see any blood or gore, so I deducted that this aisle was as good as any. Luckily, it was the aisle with the ice cream. I wrenched open one of the doors, spilling more dirt onto my dirty clothes without a care, and picked a nice, sugary treat. It felt like therapy, much better than the cigarette. The sweet cream danced on my tongue, and I almost forgot my surroundings.

CHAPTER TWELVE

Almost was a very key word.

A slender figure appeared in the corner of my eye—obviously not my father. I whipped around to see who it was. I didn't recognize him at all. He looked at me as if I were someone he knew very well and was very comfortable with. A quizzical look shifted its way to my face. The man had a perpetual smile and didn't move.

"Hi?" I said questioningly.

"Hello," he responded very cheerfully. He didn't make any movements after that. I began to get a little creeped out, so I started to turn away. All of a sudden, he grabbed my wrist, preventing me from moving. His fingers were ice cold, like they'd been in the freezer for quite some time. I looked at him with wider eyes. His grin got slightly wider and a bit crazier.

He began to squeeze on my arm with a strength I didn't know could fit in the small arms. My lungs begged to inhale and exhale at a quicker pace as I realized that this was it. I didn't have my car to hide behind, and he held the hand I'd practiced pulling out my knife with. I dropped the ice cream with the other hand, adding to the mess I'd already created on the floor. My heart started racing and my vision blurred as I became aware of my impending demise.

I wasn't going to go down without a fight. I planted my feet on the ground and attempted to tug a bit more. It was no use. I quickly tried to catalog through my options before he motioned to strike. Before I could make a decision, there was a loud crash, and I felt him tighten his grasp a bit before letting go. I instinctively shut my eyes, but only for a split second. He still stood in front of me, caught a bit off guard. Without processing the occurrence, I took the momentary pause the vampire held and used it to strike a blow directly to his chest. He fell to the floor with a thud and the figure behind him, which I hadn't noticed before, fell on him.

My dad obstructed the view of the vampire, but I could hear every sickening—but disgustingly satisfying—crunch as his fists contacted with bone, or when bone contacted with the linoleum floor. My dad was growling incoherent things repeatedly until it was replaced with heavy huffing. Soon, the whole market became as silent as when we walked in. The vampire wasn't moving, and my dad mirrored that, only moving to breathe. I stared at the frozen scene for a moment, watching the blood on the floor seep into my vision.

"I doubt he's dead," my dad stated emotionless. I couldn't tell if he was telling the truth, or trying to comfort me—or himself. He got up from the vampire and dusted off. He couldn't get off the blood that had covered the fabric of his pants, but he acted like he didn't notice. I looked around. There was ice cream all around and covering my shoes. Shining glass littered the floor, explaining the crash. My dad had slammed one of the freezer doors on his back. The vampire was bloody and bruised. The damage would have killed a human in an excruciating painful way, but my dad was right. We had no idea what they could survive.

"Come on," he said, "let's go." I said nothing, still shocked by the situation. I picked out another container of ice cream. It seemed to compliment the bag of chips my dad had found. My dad lit another cigarette in the middle of the store. I was about to say something, but I realized that it didn't really matter, considering we were the only living humans in the store. All of the social graces seemed to be thrown out the window, anyway—even though I really hadn't talked to another human to confirm. While it was also the law, the trashed store told me that no one was enforcing any laws.

He arrived at the door and put out his cigarette quickly. He then took full force through the doorway and sprinted forward. I immediately followed and we thoughtlessly made it to the SUV, watching my dad constantly look back at me. I didn't know where I'd be if my dad hadn't been there. I might've been dead. When we climbed into the vehicle, my dad locked the door and started speeding off immediately. He didn't say anything, and I began thinking back to the fight. It gave me a chill down my spine, knowing that they could be anywhere. My hands grasped onto the armrest of their own accord, rooting me to my seat. My heart beat in sync with my dad's speed, causing my breath to stagger. *They could be anywhere...* I repeated. I inhaled slowly and gradually turned around to check the backseat. My body told me that, without a doubt, there was evil lurking behind me.

Fortunately, my body was wrong. There was absolutely nothing back there. I faced forward again and breathed a sigh of relief, but the paranoia started seeping back into my veins, prompting me to check again and again on the short ride back to the dealership.

As the building came into view on the horizon, I felt a small sense of ease. It wasn't home, it wasn't safe, and it wasn't comfortable; it was familiar, and that was the only comfort I needed.

As we got closer, everything looked the same. The sun was beginning to set, and the clock was counting us down. I put my foot on my own imaginary gas pedal, urging us forward, racing against the laws of space and time. I stared at the dealership's back, trying to pull it closer to us.

As we began to get around to the front, I saw the undisturbed peace of the mostly glass structure. I could see inside and longed to be there. My thoughts stopped when the glass suddenly shattered. The pieces fell in slow motion, striking my eyes with reflections of the setting sun. Every inch it fell, I could feel myself slipping closer into a dark pit of insecurity and danger. My dad slammed on the brakes, and we swerved a bit with a screech before stopping. I was infinitely glad that we'd both put on our seatbelts in such an odd time.

We sat in silence and fear before noticing the cause of the destruction. There were pale, young figures slyly congregating around the building. Only a few moments passed before they found another thing to occupy their time: us.

"Go!" I shouted without thinking. My dad was much ahead of me. He pulled a turning maneuver that I thought was only possible in movies, using the ice to his advantage, and took off down the road in a flash.

Although he drove obviously without destination, he drove with purpose. His eyes were locked ahead, only taking quick, cursory glances at roads before turning into them. He leaned forward, toward the wheel, gripping it with an intensity that could've broken bones.

I looked behind us, and they weren't

following anymore, but my dad kept speeding forward. He kept silent, always moving ahead.

The houses grew larger and more menacing, getting darker and darker as the sun finally set. Most lights weren't on, and many of the street lamps were in disrepair. Soon, we were in eighty-five percent darkness, plunging darker with every passing hour. Every time I would see a light in a window, I would stare into that window like I could force normality into it. I would see a family sitting on a couch, watching an animated movie and eating popcorn that was buttered somewhere between artery-clogging and thunder thighs. I was with my dad on the way home from a road trip in Florida. I'd had a fun time, but I was tired and ready to go home. I'd met a girl, and we exchanged numbers, but I lost it in a drawer at the hotel. I got out and walked around the van, getting a pop from the machine, and drank it in seconds. I grabbed another quarter from the grass and put it in the slot, waiting for a strawberry milkshake. Instead, more pop cans came from the slot. There were quite a few pooling on the floor, growing and becoming the same height as me. It stopped, and so did I. I was frozen to the spot, my mouth not moving. I felt a wind on my left side as I stared at the pile of sugary comfort I couldn't grasp. Then, a vampire jumped out of the pile, claws plunging straight forward, right into my heart.

I was jolted awake. Sweat stung the edges of my eyes, and I felt instantly cold, even though my dad had the heat on full blast. I didn't know when my body decided that it was okay to sleep without my permission, but when I looked at the clock, it was about three-thirty. Judging by the almost pitch-black, it was the early hours of the morning still, and definitely not the afternoon. I looked ahead and could only see the bit that the headlights illuminated. We were driving in a very desolate area, surrounded by fields unused in the winter. There weren't any signs and was no indication of any houses around. I looked at my dad. He held the same position he had when we made our escape. He still leaned over the wheel and still had his eyes locked forward. I looked through the windshield, hoping I could see the destination he saw, but I could only see a few feet of the road ahead of us and the white plunging the rest of the view into uncertainty. While I'd slept, winter had finally taken its grasp on the weather. Ice was everywhere in the air, littering the region with snow.

"Where are we?" I asked, only trying to keep my mind off of what was outside the SUV.

"New Prague, I think," he responded without moving his gaze a centimeter.

"Oh," I said, not knowing how to keep the conversation going. Eventually, after many minutes of eerie silence, I continued, "Where are we going?"

"Nowhere," he answered.

I almost liked that reply. I wanted to go

to Nowhere, wherever it didn't exist. I wanted to cease to have to exist and let the rest of the world deal with what I'd unleashed upon it. I wanted to end all of my mistakes in one single trip, allowing all of my worries and fears fade away somewhere far from where I was.

But Nowhere didn't exist.

But I didn't want to go there—not really. I thought about my dad, hunched over the steering wheel, eyes peeled and red with concentration in the early hours of the morning. I thought about shaking hands with Jack and how I might never see him again. I remembered comforting Hannah after her parents shooed her away, seemingly not caring about her safety. I remembered spending a few moments full of passion in Alicia's room, with my skin on fire and made of ice at the same time. I saw the last time I ever saw my mom's face, sitting in her car, not looking at me. All these people I knew, few as they were, still existed, and I had to fight to exist with them, for however long it took.

Eventually, the sun began to rise, lighting the road a bit. It was still impossible to see farther than ten feet ahead of me, but my dad kept pushing ahead—wherever ahead was. My dad's muscles began to relax, including the ones holding his eyes open. His eyes were thick with red lines, and barely open.

"Tom," he said suddenly, "talk to me so I don't fall asleep."

"About what?" I asked. I didn't want to talk

about anything that was happening. I just wanted my dad to drive until we could forget it all.

"I don't care," he responded.

"Umm..." I looked around the car, looking for anything to be conversation, but it was empty. The road was barren with nothing visible in sight. I put my hands to my pockets. The knife was still there, and I thought about asking my dad if I'd really seen my mom. In reality, I knew the answer. I kept searching my pockets and found the bank statements. "So, I was in your room..." I started. My dad grunted in disapproval. "I found these...bank statements...with my name on them."

He sighed. "I was hoping you wouldn't find those until you turned eighteen. It was going to be your birthday present. I've been saving up so you could buy some video equipment."

"Oh," I said. "Not for college, like a normal parent?"

"Well," he explained, "I want you to go to college, but I want you to want to go to college more. I wanted you to do something you enjoyed, and if the better equipment meant you could make a living easier, I was willing to do it."

I didn't say anything after that. All I thought was that I had the best dad in the world.

When we finally reached a gas station, we still hadn't spoken. I felt selfish for trying to take my dad away. He'd been saving away money he could've used for a better house or a better television, just so I could follow my silly dreams. I tried to take him away from where he grew up and tried to crush his hopes of seeing those he missed, just so I wouldn't be alone.

My dad filled up the tank in the cold, not letting it show that he was freezing. He acted as if it were a sunny day outside, not pelting snow. I wanted to stand out there with him and tell him that I'd promise to be there for him, like he is for me, but my body wouldn't move. I didn't know if it was because of the cold, from my fear, or simply from my guilt, but I just couldn't budge.

I eventually took out my phone to distract my focus, only to find it dead and useless. At some point, the tank finally filled, and my dad ran into the store quickly. I couldn't see inside, but I was sure that it looked just as bad as the one I'd stopped at. I sat in my seat and looked around at the blanket crowding around the SUV, enclosing it and smothering it. It almost made me feel safer, like I couldn't be seen, and my dad and I were in a whole other world, away from the danger and away from my mistakes. But I knew that we weren't far from death. We just hid under the bed as he knocked at our bedroom door.

All of a sudden, there was a literal knock at my door. My heart jumped out of my chest as I swore. My dad was standing next to my window with arms full of goodies. I quickly opened the door as he dumped them all into my lap, enough to send a lot tumbling to the floor. Nothing spilled, but I wasn't sure how much I'd care if something did. From my knees to the bottom of my shoes was filthy from spilled food, dirt, and dried blood. I hadn't changed clothes in days and it didn't bother me.

My dad stumbled into the driver's seat and shivered. He said, "A bit nippy out." I gave a nervous laugh, but I didn't feel like I could have fun anymore. My dad, however, gave a bellowing laugh from his chest and refused to notice that I wasn't having as good of a time as he was. He popped open an energy supplement and downed it in a second. "Let's go."

I stayed silent, drowning in the pool at my pity party.

My dad backed out of the station and thrust onto the road. He started talking, but I couldn't focus my attention on him. I simply stared out into the snow, pelting the windshield like little daggers.

It must've been an hour or so before I finally registered a, "Tom? Tom?"

I looked over at my dad. He kept his focus on the road, but he frequently looked at me, waiting for a response. "Hm?"

"What's wrong?" he asked. I should've been the one asking him what was wrong. His eyes were droopy, his hands were shaking, and his skin was as white as the snow in front of us. He trembled in his seat slightly. I probably wouldn't have noticed if it were someone I didn't know, but I subconsciously memorized my dad's normal body movements. These tremors, as small as they were weren't normal. I didn't know whether it was the cold, even though steaming air was pelting us from the vents, or if it was fear or sadness—or just plain exhaustion—, but I had to help him.

As much as I dreaded what I was going to say, I knew that it would be the right thing. "I want to go home," I told him. I may have wanted to go home for him, but the rest of it was a lie. We were returning into the thick of the storm, the starting point. Staying physically safe was going to be difficult, and probably impossible, but I couldn't just sit in the passenger's seat while my dad slowly ripped his heart out of his chest.

"Okay, Tom," he said in a soft, unwavering voice. In his eyes, though, I saw them sparkle with half a tear of joy.

Considering how long we'd driven, it took an unbelievably short time to return to Eden Prairie. I assumed my dad had never wanted to fully leave and simply circled around the city until it was deemed safe. The snow was thick as ever, leading me to question whether the clock within the car was correct. It said it was the wee hours of the morning, but it looked more like eight at night. There was no trace of the sun left, and visibility was reduced to only a few feet around in each direction.

My head whipped around in all directions down every street as we drove slowly, navigating the familiar roads we couldn't see. I gambled that we wouldn't even see the danger when it came up and broke through our back window. Or our windshield. Or the passenger's side window. Or my dad's window. I increased my own heartbeat, scaring myself almost into whiplash.

I studied the scenes as intently as I could, taking in everything, looking hard enough to push the wall of invisibility a bit farther back, revealing broken houses, smashed cars, and large spots on the ground that were, very obviously, bodies and scenes of struggle. The scene was almost like a nuclear wasteland—or at least, that's what it reminded me of. There was no life anywhere to be seen—only destruction. The ground was littered with garbage, blanketed by snow, and frozen solid.

I continued to take in the scene around me, so changed even from twenty-four hours ago. I knew—somewhere deep in the darkest pits of my mind—that all of the precautionary measures these innocent people had taken had been ineffective. There was almost nothing left of our city. There was only despair and cracked wood. I didn't even fully register when my dad said, "Tom." The SUV was slowing down, which was only barely perceptible against the snail-like speed it had been going. I didn't fully want to pay attention yet; I was too busy looking at the destroyed neighborhood.

"Tom," he said a bit more urgently. I tore my eyes away from the scene to follow his gaze in front of us. Several feet ahead, almost behind the wall of visibility, was a house. It wasn't a house anymore, though. The building now sat about two feet tall. The area was so concentrated with debris that it formed a solid block on the foundation. It was hard to tell what any one thing on the lot was, not only through the blistering snowstorm, but the items on the ground were so mangled and torn that I didn't think that anything could be salvaged.

I hoped my highest hopes that no one was inside that house when it happened. There was no chance of survival. But, looking at the trees out front, I knew that no one had been in that house. My stomach dropped an inch every second as heat began to rise to my face. Chills ran up my spine as if I were standing outside, pelted by the frozen drops of deadly water, instead of inside the SUV.

My house was destroyed, broken beyond any method of repair. Not just that, but it was gone —forever. With as much as I'd wanted to leave less than forty-eight hours earlier, I guessed that I had assumed that I'd come back. I didn't know what I had expected to happen. Had I thought that we'd just leave and hide out somewhere sunny for a while? That we could just come back in a few weeks when the heat died down, and we could live life normally again? I cursed myself for being so naive, so idiotic. I was a dreamer, shown obviously by the video I'd destroyed the world with. Now, I had destroyed myself with my dreams.

And that was when a part of me broke. I began to cry. I looked away from my dad, hoping he was too wrapped up in the house's destruction to notice. I wanted to be strong. I wanted to be as I'd always been—stoic, unfeeling, nonchalant, and masculine. I know it was stupid to give in to the norms of society, but it still felt wrong for men to cry. Although I'd seen my dad do the same days earlier, it still didn't sit right. I felt like a woman.

I tried to dry them up as quickly as I could, but I was finally letting out the last few days in a series of hot, salty drops of water. Everything I'd known was represented by that house. It collapsed within itself, leaving nothing that could be fixed. Nothing was recognizable, and nothing was the same. It was all dangerous, and I couldn't go anywhere I'd previously felt safe. The worst of it was that it was entirely my fault. Everything that had happened in the past few days—the lives lost, the dreams shattered, and the destruction—was all because of me. I gritted my teeth and clenched my fists. I attempted to will the tears to stop flowing, but they only slowed, still trickling down my face, dripping onto my nose, making the whole situation a mess.

I dried my eyes on my sleeve and looked forward, not daring to look any farther at my dad. No one, not even my father, could see me cry. My eyes still burned, but the water stayed at its conception in my eyes, stinging them a bit. My vision was slightly blurred and shook with my staggered breathing. I fumbled with my hands, trying to find something to hold onto to keep my calm rooted to my consciousness. I tried to become aware of everything around me, desperate to find something, anything to keep the tears from escaping again. I felt a faint prick from my pocket, one that had probably been there for a while, but it was so faint that I hadn't noticed it much until now.

It was my cigarette box. I thrust my hand in my pocket, imagining inhaling the smoke, letting it wash down my throat, and pumping through my veins. My skin would become light and my heart's beats would become tangible. Before I could grasp the box and pull one out, my hand hit something cold and hard. It wasn't a lighter; that was in my other pocket. I pulled it out to find the shiny handle, glinted with shimmering metal. The knife I'd received from my mother rested in my open palm, right in front of my face. My eyes began to burn again, thinking of the mother I hadn't really known, but the tears stopped there. My heartbeat echoed in my ears, and, for a moment, the world moved in a slow manner. Even though I hadn't heard from my mother in years, this knife, cold and stuck in my hand, told me, in words whispering straight into my bloodstream, that she still loved me. She would soon know that I was here, waiting for her. She would come back soon.

The thought energized me enough to put the cigarette out of my mind for now. I looked back ahead at my old house and clenched the knife in my hand as tightly as I could. I was finally ready to face the world ahead of me. My dad, myself, and my mom were here with me. Even if I couldn't see her, I could feel her, pushing onward with us, ready to take on what came next.

CHAPTER THIRTEEN

We sat at the house for a while in silence. I don't know if we were both willing it to piece itself back together, but I knew that I was. My eyes pierced through the snow, scanning the destruction for something, for anything that could make this alright. But I found nothing. Everything blended and meshed together to create something horrific and black. The pile seemed to seep and grow shorter with every passing second. Everything was disappearing, not physically, but the more I looked at it, the more we seemed to drift further away from where I grew up, where my dad grew up, and from where it all started.

The drifting stopped suddenly when I saw movement. It must've been a raccoon or something scavenging the wreckage for anything able to be eaten. I knew he wouldn't find anything. The destruction was much too bad. Oblivious, the movement continued. Looking closer, the movement was far too big to be a raccoon, maybe a large dog. Or maybe...?

I had a sudden flash of déjà vu. It was just like my dream. Out of the pile of rubble shot out a humanoid figure that I knew instantly was a vampire. The movements were fast and powerful. It headed straight toward us, but my dad, even in his tired, depressed stupor, was much too fast for her. He sped forward, turning the wheel as far to the left as he could. He was obviously pushing the gas pedal to the floor. We weren't going quite as fast as I'd like, but the second we hit a small spot of the road that the wheels could grasp for a moment, we set off into dangerous speeds. In all honesty, the speed was probably safer than what was back there.

My hand grasped down harder on the knife in my hand, and I felt a sharp sting. I looked down at my shaking hand to find the knife open. I must've opened it when the vampire jumped out. Now, I'd cut my hand open, spilling blood onto my shirt. It was bleeding quite a lot. I grabbed some napkins from the pile of garbage food my dad took from the gas station. I pressed them onto the wound and watched the blood pool onto the white napkins. I looked at the knife partially hidden by the dirty napkins. It was still open, and I could see my reflection in the blood-stained knife. It was hard to recognize it as myself. There were lines all leading to bloodshot eyes. My facial hair began to grow in and dotted my face. My hair was matted with dirt, and my face was covered in it as well. I looked older, much older. Not like when Hannah dressed me, but a different older—a deeper one. It was the kind you'd see at a veteran's home. Even though some of those men were fifty, maybe sixty, they'd seen enough life and death to be alive for one hundred and fifty years. That had become me.

"What happened to your hand?" my dad asked.

I didn't look up at him when I answered, "I cut myself on the knife." I was too enraptured by my own reflection. It seemed so foreign, so unusual to me. The napkins became soaked in blood, but I couldn't move. I didn't recognize anything in front of me. My hand didn't even seem to be my own.

I heard a rustling, followed by the click of a lighter. My dad was trying to light a cigarette while driving speeds clearly over seventy miles an hour in a snowstorm. As much as I understood the need for the calming effects of nicotine, it was dangerous.

"Dad, you're going to—" I started.

There was a jolt as we side-swiped another car. There was a sharp pain in my left leg, and as I looked down, I found that I stabbed myself. I took a sharp intake of oxygen, and the pain pulsed strongly in my leg. I let out a gasp of pain. I grasped the handle of the knife and slid it out of the wound, rippling pain throughout my leg. My dad didn't notice. He had lost control of the SUV, and was trying to regain it. We hit another car as we swerved to another side. The impact shot pain, starting from the wound and up the muscles throughout my body. When it reached my sliced hand, another wave of pain electrified my body.

My hands instantly grasped each other, pushing on my leg, trying to squeeze out the pain. I took deep breaths, willing myself not to look up as I felt the SUV thrash from side to side like a bull. Every pull from every direction was like the knife sliced through my skin again and again, not only in the wounds, but cutting deep inside, right into my lungs. Every breath was a rush of dread as I locked my eyes shut, waiting for it to end.

I focused on the quick, even beats of my heart, thinking of nothing else. I forgot the pain. I forgot the jerking. I even forgot the video, the attacks, and the death and destruction surrounding me. All I allowed myself to think of was thumpthumpthumptumpthump. With the speed and the power behind each beat, it was amazing that it calmed me. I was completely oblivious as to when my dad regained control, but after several moments lost in broken consciousness, we were heading calmly down a road I couldn't recognize.

"Where...do we go?" I finally asked.

"I don't know," he said very, very quietly.

After countless minutes of silence, only broken by the sounds of breathing and the hammering of ice on the SUV, we began to make it into the richer part of town. The neighborhood seemed more intact than the rest of the town, but it was just as eerie—if not more. The only thing I could see that was broken was the gate, meant to keep out the undesirables. At one point, that might've been us, but there were scarier things on the world's plate. Now, it didn't keep either out.

We slowed down, unsure of where to go next. Every house was dark and lifeless. While we knew these houses would have everything we needed, and probably anything we'd ever want, we didn't stop. The security would be damn-near impossible with all of the sophisticated alarm systems any other kind of safety they could gather up with their money. Regardless of how void they were of life, the engineering inside could potentially get us arrested. I wondered if the police were even around to catch us. We could've probably broken into one, but we didn't. Whether or not we'd get caught, it wasn't the kind of person I was—no matter how much I wanted it. Looting a destroyed gas station was one thing, but stealing from someone—a real live person—was something else entirely. I wasn't about to throw away everything my dad taught me just for a moment of material goods.

But still, I imagined how it would be to finally live in the life of (stolen) luxury—imported food and wine, electronics as far as the eye could see, the highest definition of television—just like Alicia. I thought back to her, and my heart began to beat quickly again, sending a spark of pain from my leg again. I tried not to focus on it, locking my mind onto Alicia. While it seemed to make the pain worse, it put my mind at ease. I tried not to think of where she was or if she was okay. Instead, I just focused on her, and how I felt, and how it was the first time we met.

It was a few years ago, but I remembered it very clearly.

On the first day of school, Jack and I had our first period together, as we often had. We picked a lot of the same classes, not fully intentionally, but it just seemed to happen that way. Jack and I were talking and laughing—not about the movie, but something very meaningless and stupid. It was before the movie had taken a hold of my mind. It was before everything had gotten complicated and difficult.

Everyone sat wherever they liked, forming their own cliques. Jack's friends, the jocks, sat by him, but he didn't talk to them at the time besides the "hey" and a fist pound. He was too busy talking to me. It was great to have a friend like Jack. No matter how popular he became, he was my friend, choosing me over his jock buddies—most of the time. It was all okay, though. He had his friends, and I had my own things.

The bell rang, and no one paid any notice. The teacher hadn't started yet, but slowly everyone began to quiet down and slowly turn their bodies forward. It was funny how people were like sheep, one following another, not quite sure why. When nearly everyone was silent and facing the board, the teacher started with roll call, as most of the teachers did. Again, just like sheep, we all looked at the names that called "here"—or the ones who thought they were cool when they said, "yo"—in unison. But there was one name that held the heads of a few boys, including mine and Jack's.

We'd never met Alicia before; she must've just moved. Jack quietly uttered the exact same word I was thinking: "Damn!" This girl was gorgeous. Her hair was long, straight, and incredibly shiny. It looked as if she had her own personal stylist just for the mornings. Her clothes were ironed, matched, and sexy. She looked like a schoolgirl—or, more like a girl in the "naughty schoolgirl" costume. Her skin was smooth and flawless, and she was every boy's fantasy.

"I call her," Jack said quietly to me.

I glared at him. "No way, dude," I stated. "You can't have Hannah and her."

"Sure I can."

"Bastard," I grumbled, looking forward. I knew that in a battle for a girl, Jack would always win. Still, my eyes strayed away, and I looked at her. Her eyes were locked forward, cold. It was almost as if she didn't know that there were eight boys eying her down. Or, I guessed, she was making a point not to notice. She wanted them all to know that she was above their games. Maybe, just maybe, she was above Jack's games, too.

That thought carried me through months

of trying to make conversation with her. She was frigid and short, but it was farther than Jack ever got. Not that he seemed to care that she didn't like him, but it definitely bothered him that she'd talk to me and not him.

I had to have asked her out ten times before she finally said yes, in December. It was just a week before Christmas, and the snow fell softly on the ground, covering the sidewalk. I bundled up as much as I could and walked down the street to where we agreed to meet. The streets were scarcely lit by street lamps, but it wasn't a far walk. She was there waiting for me in front of the shop. She looked just as beautiful as she had the first day I met her. She still kept a look of apathy on her face, but this time, I hoped there was something underneath.

We said our hellos, and she led me inside the coffee chain. It was a bit run down, a bit dirty, and a bit cold, but Alicia seemed to radiate something in the air. I didn't really care where we were—just that I was here with her. That it wasn't Jack getting the girl again.

I got a black coffee, just to show her that I was tough, too. It was bitter, but I liked it. It was warm, and it kept me on my toes. I was determined to get through her thick skin, and find out what was underneath.

It took at least a half hour before she showed a flicker of interest. I told her that I wanted to be a director. It was like an actress change. Suddenly, this cold, unfeeling girl was drilling me with questions and devouring every word I said. But it wasn't just about movies, but it was about everything: what I liked and didn't like, what I have and haven't done, my parents' names... I didn't even get to ask any questions about her.

After another hour about me, she got up and said, "Come on. Let's do something fun."

She pulled on my arm. I stayed where I was and asked, "What's with the sudden change of character?"

She gave me a quizzical look, and I explained, "You've spent this whole date—this whole semester trying to keep me off your back, and now, suddenly, you're interested? What's the deal?"

She sighed very slowly. "I guess, I was never really listening," she disclosed. "I always thought you were just like all of them. You and your buddies wanted to see who could get with the hot, new girl—yes, I heard you and your friend talking. You would have no personality, and just wanted to prove a point or win a bet.

"It's how my life has always been, moving and seeing the same thing over and over again. I'd always try out a few persistent guys, hoping one was different. But they never were. They all want to be a basketball player or an accountant. None of them had any dreams that weren't given to them by their parents, or the television.

"But, you—you want to be a director. You

want to make people believe in the impossible. You want to show them emotions that will make them cry and laugh at the same time. You want to be something other than a faceless crowd member, even if you may never be seen."

I was quiet for a moment. She pressed on, "Why are you interested in me?"

"I-I..." I didn't know if I had an answer for her. She was gorgeous, yes, but I knew there was something else.

"Come on," she told me. "It's only fair." She scowled at me, waiting for an answer.

"I guess..." I drew the word out, stalling. I wanted to dictate it just right, not to make a fool of myself. "...you're the first girl here who doesn't play the games."

I expected her to ask me what the games were, but she didn't. She only replied, "You're right. I don't play those games. Now, come on." She coaxed me out of the shop and into the freezing wind and snow. I left my coffee on the table and instantly regretted it. The wind blew into the holes of my apparel, and I desperately wanted to get back inside.

"Aren't you cold?" I asked, looking at her get-up. She wore long socks with a skirt, a small jacket and a scarf that she didn't bother tying.

"Very," she replied, looking in her purse, "but I've got something to warm up with." As she said it, she pulled out a bottle of cheap tequila.

My eyes grew wide. I'd only drank once,

and I was eager to continue. However, I was incredibly wary about how public we currently were. "Shouldn't we do that somewhere more, you know, private?"

"Here, come to our temporary apartment. We'll drink on the way," she said with a smile that made my heart beat in all parts of my body. She took my hand, just as cold as mine, and pulled me down an alley. I breathed a sigh of relief as we were fading out of sight.

She continued walking as she unscrewed the cap. She took a small gulp and shook her head. She kept her mouth and her eyes closed as she handed the bottle to me. I looked to my right and my left and only found brick walls. I deemed it safe and took a small sip. It tasted god-awful, and I almost coughed it up, but I was determined to keep it going.

I took another sip before I gave it back. My eyes squeezed shut, and I hoped Alicia could lead me properly. The terrible taste set itself on repeat over and over in my mind until I noticed the burning in my chest—a good burning. It warmed me and loosened my grip on feeling. I finally opened my eyes and walked slower with Alicia.

She handed the bottle back to me, and I took another sip. It was still just as bad, but it didn't leave the bad feelings as it had before. My eyes stayed open as we walked, and we began to share the bottle in a more rapid succession. My tension washed out of my body and over the pristine snow on the ground. Time started to flow more freely, and the world didn't seem so tethered anymore. The only thing that seemed stuck in one place was Alicia's hand in mine.

I barely remembered the walk back to Alicia's apartment. I just remember laughing and walking. I didn't even remember which apartment complex Alicia lived in or what door we took to get in. I did remember what happened when we got to her room. She began to kiss me. We were still freezing from being outside, but the tequila clashed with the ice, and made everything a sweet in-between.

Her lips were hard, but inviting. I could feel her hands running along my body, but I felt nothing else. Nothing else in the world existed. We were both here, kissing and enveloped in each other. But, once we hit the bed, that's where my mind threw up its hands and refused to remember any more.

When I woke up, I was in my bed—at my house. I stared up at the ceiling with a slightly spinning head. It was hard to figure out what happened last night. I didn't remember coming home, and I didn't remember what had transpired after Alicia and I left the coffee shop. It would be days before I actually pieced together everything I would ultimately remember.

I had flashes of us kissing, pressing our bodies together, but it was nothing concrete, and it was nothing clear enough to distinguish between dreams and reality. But those scenes made me feel —not only for Alicia, but for something new and exciting. I instantly dove around my room for a pencil and paper. I began scribbling on the page, and, in the end, it was the hoax movie.

I stared at the paper and knew it was something big. I spent the whole day planning it out, and the next day telling Jack. Eventually, Hannah was recruited, and the whole project began to unfold into what it was today.

But I still thought about Alicia. It was still a few months before she was on board with the project. After that night, she pulled herself away from me again. She refused to acknowledge that night—not quite denying it, but she wouldn't give me any details. We became distant friends, and not becoming real friends until the movie began to take pace. I wondered what happened, and longed to have that night back. I was so happy, and she made my skin tingle with every touch.

One day, I asked her, point-blank, if we had sex that night. She said, "Yes." She didn't speak to me at all for the rest of that day. I worked my brain so hard to try and recall that night, but it was in vain. So, I never gave up hope, wishing to relive that night with her.

Another snap of pain from my wounds jerked me back to the present. My injured hand clenched together into a fist, sending more pain into my nervous system. I desperately began to work my eyes to their best, trying to find an escape into something that would stop the pain. In the distance, my eyes focused on two small figures up ahead. They looked like guards standing at the edge of a house, but that was impossible. I couldn't grasp what they were through the snow.

Without any warning, the car pulled to one side sharply. Without time to ask what happened, the windshield flew inward, little shards piercing my skin. The pain ran down my face, causing me to let out a small, painful shriek. I felt nails scraping the skin on my arm, and I took in a horrible breath. In the back of my consciousness, I could hear an angry snarl. My vision was blurred, and I couldn't see anything, but I knew what was happening. My body ached, and the sound dulled. I couldn't go on. This was finally it, and I almost let go.

There was a loud snap and all sound stopped. Movement ceased. Quickly, my door was yanked open. I heard a few voices muttering, but I didn't pay attention. The pain was unbearable. I stopped the fading for a moment, and fought to come back, but the struggle was too much. Soon enough, I pulled myself away from the real world for a while and took on a dreamless sleep.

CHAPTER FOURTEEN

I woke up, still hurting. I tried to move, but I was very stiff. The room was warm and quiet, except for some quiet music in the background. My eyes gradually opened themselves, afraid of where I could possibly be now. My house was gone; my dad's office was gone. I knew that I was in a bed, but the owner was a mystery. I only saw a white ceiling above me at first and was almost unwilling to continue looking. I wanted to close my eyes and finally quit. My body hurt, and it didn't want to move. My friends were missing, and my life was upside-down.

But I had to keep fighting. I had to find my friends, rebuild my life, and fix what I'd done. I forced my gaze around and found myself in a very familiar bedroom. It took a few minutes for my vision to return to normal, but it cleared simultaneously with a very sharp pain that woke me up fully. Shooting to a sitting position only made the pain worse. I let out a pain-filled grunt.

A gentle hand pushed me by my shoulder

back down to the bed. The touch was incredibly painful as well, but it also calmed me. "It's alright," I heard an incredibly familiar female voice tell me.

My mind raced and I put the puzzle pieces together. "Hannah?" I asked groggily.

I turned my head in her direction. She looked beautiful. Although it had only been a few days, I missed her so much. "Yeah," she replied, patting my hair. She smiled, showing her dazzling white teeth, and she looked like an angel. She looked a bit disheveled and stressed, but, all in all, she looked okay.

"What-what happened?" I asked, remembering only a few of the details.

"Hm..." She thought for a moment before responding, "Well, you have half a windshield of glass in your face, deep infected cuts on your forearm, hand, and leg, and a slightly bruised skull..."

"Oh," was all I said. My head tried to sort through the events through the throbbing pain. I didn't remember much after being saved. Looking back on it, I should've known that we had been approaching Hannah's house. Those guards... I tried to sort, but the pain made me stop. Instead, I vocalized the thought. "Who were..." I started, but I let my brain trail off to save energy.

"The guards," she explained, taking the time to look toward the closed door. I heard a cough on the other side, and I realized that there must be one on the other side. "My parents didn't want to leave their *possessions*"—the sneer in her voice was almost tangible—"so we got someone to protect us and our things." Her gaze was fixed toward the heart of the house. Her hair fell down the back of her head like a golden waterfall, and I couldn't help but stare and ponder the life she'd had over the past few days.

The hurdles money could simply float over were astonishing. Instead of running, Hannah simply sat at home. "Living in the lap of luxury while the rest of us risk our lives out there, huh?" I joked. There was a bit of truth in the joke, though. Everything my dad and I had been through, mentally and physically, was horrific, and she just got to sit in her house, do what she wanted, and be safe.

She turned to me with a hard look. "I would hardly call it luxury, Tom." She sighed and her face softened. "It's lonely here. My parents and I never had a connection. They never even paid attention until I began cheerleading and acting dumb. The only other option is the guards, but they won't let their attention leave our safety for a second. Jack is missing, and you won't answer your phone. I was afraid I would have to run away...not that I'd get far." Her face then turned to the window, pelted with snow and icing over. Her eyes shined, and I felt a sudden urge to get closer to her.

I'm delusional, I thought. *This is my best friend's girlfriend. It must be the injuries. I've never seen her in this way before.* Without another thought, I blurted, "Am I on any drugs?" I didn't realize how bad it sounded until it hung between us. It hadn't even been a fully-formed idea before I vocalized it.

It did entice a little chuckle out of her, complimented with a smile that could break your heart. "Just some ibuprofen. We aren't doctors here," she responded, still smiling.

Just the injuries then... I assured myself. Desperate to keep talking, I asked, "So, what have you been up to, cooped up in here?"

She scrunched her face up a bit before answering. "Nothing really. Movies—all of the channels are dead, making up my hair in different ways, trying to contact Jack..." A sad note pinged in her voice. I guessed that he didn't tell Hannah where he went.

"Oh, he went south with his family," I explained. Her expression didn't change at all. "He said he'd be in contact when he could..." I continued.

"Oh." It seemed to be a popular word today. Every time it was spoken, it echoed the desperation and hopelessness of the situation. "So, why haven't you been answering your phone?" she asked distractedly.

I pulled a quizzical look on my face. "It never rang..." I took the painful effort to yank it out of my pocket. It was off for some reason. I tried to turn it back on, but it wouldn't. "Must be dead," I remarked. It didn't even cross my mind to plug it in, or even bring the charger along.

She got up. "I'm sure I've got the same charger..." She rummaged around the messy room. I just then realized how disorganized the room had become since the last time I'd been in it. There was so much space that it could've hardly been the disaster my room was. *Was*, my mind repeated again, remembering that everything I owned was in my destroyed house. Except for what I left in my car, which I was unaware of its condition.

"Redecorating?" I asked, trying to coax out her smile again.

It was unsuccessful. "I've been a bit frustrated with my parents and their money." The resentment she held with some of those words was as sharp as daggers, ready to slit the throat of a metaphorical animal.

"It's okay," I told her. "I'm sure they'll come around."

She found the cord and her moves became jerky and forceful. "No," she replied, handing me the charger. "This is how they are. They both grew up in wealthy families, and the wealth was passed onto them. They barely have to work at all, and they never knew what it was like to not have things."

"But you grew up this way," I pointed out as I plugged in my phone. I didn't want to tell her that she seemed to be getting more and more like them over the years. She wasn't anywhere close now, but I'd known her since she was little, and it was a gradual change.

She shook her head and handed me a phone charger. "I don't know what happened to me. I guess it's the school, and my friends."

"Your friends?" The only friends other than our core group of four I could recall were her cheerleading girls and her slew of boyfriends trailing behind her. If anything, they encouraged her to be the same way.

"Well," she replied, "more like, a friend."

"Who?" I asked.

"Well, I knew this boy, back in elementary school," she explained, not looking at me. "He came from a bit of a poorer family. Added to that, his mom left, and he didn't really have many friends, 'cause he was depressed all the time.

"But I went up to that boy. He was the only one who I hadn't shown my new, two-hundred dollar dolphin bracelet to. I just remember him sitting in the sand. He only looked at it once, and said, 'oh.' I was very confused. He got up slowly and moved to another spot, away from me and played with the sand there. I followed him and he moved.

"We seemed to do that for a few days. Everybody else was jealous of my money, which is exactly what I wanted, but it wasn't that way with that boy. But, I wanted to know why he didn't like me. One day, I left the bracelet at home and, when recess came, I just sat down in the sand next to him. We didn't say anything that first day, but I continued to sit next to him. The second day, he asked me where my bracelet was, but we didn't talk after that.

"The third day, we began talking. He talked about his dad and his mom. That third day, he said more words than he had ever said in class. He talked about how he had no friends, and almost started to cry. But, that day, I did something that no one else did. I said that I'd be his friend. We became really good friends, and I couldn't see why anyone else didn't want to be friends with him. He was really fun, he was really cute, and he was really smart. He worked on homework with me, which I had never done my homework, and he helped me realize that I was a really smart girl."

She looked at me now, almost tearing up. "That boy made me realize, for a while at least, that my parents were wrong, and I didn't have to be like them. I thought that if I was more like that boy, maybe he would kiss me. He never did, though. He was always just my friend. Soon, I noticed that my parents didn't care about my good grades or my poor friend. So, I got a boyfriend, Jack, and went back to being the dumb blonde my parents wanted.

"Deep down inside, I knew that the boy changed my life forever. Deep down, I wasn't my parents, even if I was on the outside." She sniffled a bit. "I'm still a bit in love with that boy today."

She looked down at the floor. I took my

hand and brought her face to look at mine. She tried to avert her eyes, but I held her face long enough that she couldn't help but look at me back. I looked at her, even with her red, puffy eyes, they shined like jewels. "That boy is still here," I said. "He's just waiting for that girl to come back."

"I tried, and I tried," she cried. "I always wanted to let you know that I was still in here. But Jack...and he..." She choked on her words as tears ran down her perfect cheeks. "You know, I've only ever slept with Jack," she revealed, out of place. "Those other boys are lying."

I chuckled a bit. "I don't care." I leaned over and kissed her.

I knew I always had feelings for her, ever since she sat in the sand with me and agreed to be my friend. I was shy, and I didn't think she'd kiss me. I buried them deep inside, in hopes that they would fizzle out, and die. They didn't, but lay dormant. Now, they awakened, burning my eyes and pushing my heart. Every time we were alone, I felt the pull that no one could get between, but people always tried.

My lips were tingling when we broke apart. I smiled and she smiled, and then we both laughed. It had taken us so long to finally kiss, and to finally realize that we both wanted the same thing. It felt good, like a weight that was held on my shoulders for years was lifted, when I had gotten used to it being there.

My phone buzzed. I turned my ear to it, still

holding Hannah's hand in mine. I almost didn't even look at it, but I knew I had to. Alicia, it called at me on the screen. My heart twitched a little, feeling torn between an old flame and a new heat, but I pushed it aside to be all business.

"Hello?" I told the phone. My heart raced, not knowing what she would say next. I imagined the worst of things, like how she wanted to be together, or how she had been in the window the whole time, but I never imagined what she said next.

"Tom?!" she whispered worriedly. "I need you! I'm trapped at the school! There's a vampire here, and—" I heard a little gasp and the phone dropped. I heard the sound of footsteps running off, and then heard nothing.

I stared at the phone in my hand. I had pushed all of the distress and worry away in a few simple minutes, and now it was back with a vengeance. The phone shook, but not from ringing. My heart beat loudly in my ears as the environment blurred around me. The muted sound of Hannah's voice was faint in the distance. Alicia was in trouble. I had to go save her.

I shot up and darted around the room for anything that might help. I grabbed my coat and a large book. It was the closest thing to a weapon I could see.

"What?" Hannah demanded.

Without stopping, I answered, "Alicia's at the school. She's being chased. I have to save her."

I continued to grab random things. I pulled on a girl's coat, not caring, considering nobody would see.

Hannah grabbed my arm. I instantly pulled away. "You can't go," she pleaded. "You'll get killed!"

"Alicia will get killed if I don't help her!" I argued as I walked out into the hallway. I didn't stop at all, not wanting to waste time, but I did take a wrong turn here or there. I took it in stride, not wanting to stop the determination.

"Please!" Apparently, she was right behind me, and she grabbed my arm again. I shook her off. Eventually, I reached the front door. The guards didn't stop me as I strode right into the snowstorm. The wind barreled against any exposed skin, burning on contact. It looked like ten o'clock at night, not noon, the cover was so thick. The snow may have slowed me down, but it didn't stop me. It couldn't stop me.

"Wait!" I heard Hannah scream. I could feel the tears welling in her eyes, echoed in her voice. The small gesture made me turn around. I quickly returned to the door, but didn't stop moving. The guards were stopping her.

"I can't waste any more time," I remarked, getting close to her, looking straight into her glossy eyes.

She sniffed. "You have to think about this..." she said pleadingly.

"I did."

"But, is it a good idea?" she attempted.

"Hannah," I stroked her arm. It was growing cold with the bitter wind. "Part of making a good decision is just making a decision. You can't always sit and weigh the pros and cons. There just isn't time for that. Making a good decision means sticking with your choice and dealing with what comes with it. Being able to deal with the consequences—that's making a good decision."

She sniffled again. She held out a set of keys. "The only car in the driveway," she explained. She continued to try and slow her cries while holding her head down.

I took one long look at her, not really knowing if I would ever see her again. I took her chin in my hand and made her face me again. Her liquid eyes made the rest of my body unaware of the cold around me. Her porcelain skin with a river of blonde hair captivated me enough to want to stay. But I couldn't.

I brought her red lips to meet mine for what could be the final time. It was only for a second or two, but it felt like a lifetime. Hannah was always there right next to me, and I was always distracted by Alicia or some dream. She may have been on Jack's arm a lot of the time, but she wasn't his property. She belonged to no one. She was her own woman, and she belonged with me.

The kiss broke off after what seemed like ages, but not long enough. I took the keys from her hand. "Tell my dad I love him," I told her and turned away. I went all the way to the car without turning back. It was another SUV. When I got to the car, I took a quick look at her. She was staring at me shivering, but I wasn't sure if it was from the cold or from the sadness. I quickly made my way into the car and drove off, before I let a tear roll down my check. I cursed myself for being so weak, but, in the privacy of the SUV, I let it happen. I drove mechanically to the school, looking back at what I said.

I had no idea where it came from, or even how relevant it may have been, but I could definitely see it being in one of my movies. Then, I stopped myself, wondering whether I will ever get the chance to make a movie. *Again,* I thought. As short lived as it was, everyone saw that movie. It was what I always wanted. Would I ever get to live my dreams again?

I grappled at higher speeds, forgetting about the ice on the ground until I began skidding. Surprisingly, I didn't slow down. I had to get there, and save Alicia. My mind spun in another direction as the SUV did. Who was Alicia to me? I had a simple high school crush on her for so long, and now with Hannah. *Do I love her? Which her was I referring to? When—if—I saved her, would she —*

My heart beat rapidly on my ribcage as the car sped out of control. I frantically turned at the wheel, but it did no good, as I knew it wouldn't.

I tried to remember everything I'd learned when learning how to drive, but it was no use. I was too broken. All of the adrenaline I'd acquired left me, and I was helpless. The vehicle began to tip over, and I tried my best to turn my body in the opposite direction, but the iron hold of the seatbelt prevented any harsh movement. The world turned and crashed around me. My windows broke and flew around me, just like the movie, only in slow motion. Every glinting speck of the sharp glass cut through my mind, reflecting something I'd forgotten, like the smell of my mom's things, or the first girl I kissed. My whole life and anything I'd leave behind shone into my soul and choked in my lungs. I could smell the burnt metal as it bent and twisted itself into a cage around me.

I don't know at what point I passed out, but it wasn't for very long. The vehicle was on its side, pulling me down to the passenger's side, straight onto the frozen pavement. Holding myself on the center console, I unhooked the belt. When the support left, my arm almost buckled under the weight. I looked at it and saw a bit of dirty blood trickling down from an open wound. I looked up and saw the caved in window with enough room to push out. I slowly wriggled my way out, ignoring the stings of broken glass, mixing with the pains of already existing wounds.

I jumped out of the destroyed vehicle and crashed against a large snow bank. The cold felt much better on my skin than the bleeding wounds.

The cold held me like a large embrace, wanting to pull me into its sweet darkness. My eyelids became heavy and tried to close me in. My breathing slowed and my heart followed until they were in a slow rhythm of a lullaby.

The biting cold jerked me up seconds before sleep...or worse. I looked around in the increasingly white air, turning dark. At this point, I wouldn't be able to tell you the time through the thick onslaught of crystal snow. I looked around and saw nothing familiar—or much at all, really. The only thing I could see was a crushed vehicle and a snowstorm.

I started walking in the direction the destroyed SUV was facing, not immediately recalling my destination, but I knew I needed to keep going. After walking for a bit, I remembered the phone call from Alicia and began running. I wasn't even sure that I was still going in the right direction, but she needed me. Out of anyone she could have called, or may have called, she reached out to me, and I would be there for her.

I calculated what I would do when I got there, with no weapons left. I tried to think of anything I could pick up in the school, but the cold mixed with the pain, and the pain mixed with confusion, and the confusion mixed with adrenaline, and it all ended up into one hurtful mess. I almost buckled under the pressure, but then I realized it wasn't the pressure. The wound on my leg, left by my knife was still there, unable to heal. I drove my hand in my pocket and pulled out the knife. I kept it closed tightly in my fist, secure. I had a way. *I'm going to save you, Alicia.*

I thought about Hannah, and what we had, and what all of this would mean. Who would I choose when the time came? I kept running, sliding here and there, but never breaking my stride. I didn't stop until my busy mind registered that there was something in my path. I quickly stopped in time to avoid a toppled street sign. I stopped to brush the snow off of it, hoping that I knew the street I was on. I read the sign, "Holyoke Ave". The street seemed familiar, and I should have known what it was.

It took a minute for me to realize that I was on the street of my school. I whipped around, looking, but everything was washed out and unrecognizable. I carefully began to tread into the freezing snow, trying to get close to a building, any building, to get my bearings. For a few biting steps, I couldn't see anything until a shadow loomed before me. It was a large building, plainly rectangular. Closer up, I saw faded bricks and small windows.

This was it. I made it to the school.

I quickly trudged through the snow, across the length of the bricks. I didn't know what part of the school I was at, or how far it was to the next door, but I was running out of time. The snow seemed to pile around me, slowing every step. When at last I finally reached a door, my legs were numb and barely listened to my commands. I pulled at the handle, but the door didn't budge. I rammed a shoulder against it, jarring my body. The impact left every part of my body that wasn't numb in intense pain. I tried at the door again and bellowed in frustration. I didn't have time to look for the next door. I looked at my feet, numb and housed by snow-filled boots. They were numb to the point of medication, and it gave me an idea. I gently kicked the door and felt nothing. I kicked again, harder, with nothing again. With every force left in my body, I sucked in a gulp full of air and lashed out with my foot against the glass of the door.

It produced a large hole in the bottom. I swiftly kicked at the hole until I could punch out an area for me to step through. The hallways were dark, but I knew I was in the west wing. I listened for any sign of Alicia's location, but silence greeted me back. I began taking swift, silent steps toward the heart of the school, keeping my ears open for any sign.

I reached the center of the school and held my breath, to listen for anything. At first, there was nothing. I felt alone in the vast area. The rush began to leave as dark thoughts came down. My heart dropped, wondering if I was too late. Then, just as I let the breath go, I heard a faint click coming from the arts wing. I raced in that direction, faster than I've ever gone.

I reached the wing and stopped to listen.

Again, I was greeted by the quiet. I began stepping down the hallway as soundlessly as I could. I peered into a few open doors and saw nothing. I didn't dare turn on any lights, for fear of being seen. After checking a few doors, I let out a large breath. On cue, I heard the click again. My heart continued to run away, taking my oxygen with it. I quickly turned in the direction and listened. There were slow, repeated clicks on the linoleum floor. I soon recognized them as footsteps. It sounded like a movie where the girl in the red dress walked into the ballroom, alone. The sound was amplified and echoed. Only, these steps were purposeful and directed—at me. They were slow, but I couldn't stay in one place.

I crept around a corner and held my breath, listening. The footsteps followed me without fail. I leaned my back against the cold wall and pondered my next move. As they became increasingly closer, I silently sidled across the wall until I reached another corner, and followed it. I whipped around the corner and stopped. The footsteps had stopped, no doubt listening for me. I left my breath shallow and quiet as I thought about what I could do. *Where was Alicia?* This was certainly not her. I needed to save her. I gripped the knife in my hand and squeezed it. It hurt, but it let me know that I was alive, and I could fight.

The footsteps began again in my direction, and I swore at myself for letting my breathing become loud again. With a racing heart, I continued to follow the wall to my next move. Suddenly, my right side hit a wall, and the wounds on my arm flashed with pain. I was at a dead end. I'm sure I let out a surprised gasp on impact. I felt my eyes grow wide and a sweat pool at my temples as the little clicks slowly gained the distance between us.

As if an act of the heavens, right before the shoes sounded around the corner, a loud crash came from behind it. The reverberating sound immediately identified it as the auditorium. I froze, willing, hoping the figure would turn around and focus on the crash instead. After an agonizing, slow, silent minute, the sound began heading in the opposite direction. My heart beat loudly in my ears, as I had narrowly escaped certain death. For now, I told myself. I still needed to find Alicia...

My entire body stopped breathing, beating, pumping, and thinking. That crash was probably her, struggling to get away. My heart panicked, racing at high speeds. I mentally drew up the layout of the arts wing. It was a little fuzzy, and I vowed, if everything returned to normal, I would make sure that I was more involved in school activities. The high-heeled shoes were making their way toward the main entrance of the auditorium. I calculated my position and figured —guessed—that the dressing rooms were straight ahead of me. I looked to my right, at the wall, and then to my right, at the darkened hallway. That may be my only chance to save her. I sucked in a deep breath, and, before I could think, I sprinted into the dark hallway. Without thought, I yanked open the door ahead of me, unsure of where it would lead, but wishing that it was the dressing rooms.

The smell of freshly opened makeup greeted me, and I heaved a sigh of relief. However, I didn't waste time finding the first large thing, a clothes rack, to place in front of the door. I heaved it in front of the large door and waited for the impending push against it. It never came, but I didn't wait too long for it to happen. I looked around the narrow hallway, catching my breath. It was dimly lit by a light carelessly left on from the woman's dressing room. I didn't dare waste time and peek in—not that there would be anything in there, anyway.

The hallway was short and blocked by a large black curtain. Slowly, I crept up to it and pressed an ear out. The curtain didn't betray the auditorium's sound. I crept my hand around it and pulled just enough to see into the large, dark stage. At first, I saw nothing, accompanied by the eerie silence. When my eyes began adjusting to the darkness, I could faintly see the edges of the stage. I followed the edge, giving my eyes something to focus on.

I didn't notice anything originally. It took a while for me to even see the chairs in the audience, even though I knew they were there. It still astounded me that I didn't notice the pile in the middle of the empty stage until just then. In my defense, it was dark, and the lump was black, like the stage. The outline was fuzzy, and I began thinking it was a pile of broken curtains, but the outline grew harder and more concrete the more I stared at it. It was a body.

I threw the curtain away and ran to it. I felt the arm facing up and it was cold and smooth. I saw no rising and falling of the chest. I turned the body over, closing my eyes in hopes that if I didn't see Alicia's face, it wouldn't be her. I imagined every possible way her face could be contorted, frozen forever. She was scared or screaming. She was peacefully asleep. Her lips formed my name in her last breath. I felt myself turn the body over in my hands, light and lifeless. I slowly opened my eyes to take in the face before me, bracing for the worst. In the initial look, it could have been anybody. My eyes had readjusted themselves again, and I had to wait for them to return.

When my vision began to process the face, something wasn't right about it. I soon realized that it wasn't Alicia. It didn't seem to be anyone I knew, extensively or passively. It actually wasn't anybody. It was a life-sized doll. The detail was incredible, but I wondered why it was here. *In Alicia's clothes...* I noticed. I looked around the dark stage. It was so eerily silent. The darkness made the room looked like it went on forever. I looked back at the doll, only for a second before a loud voice penetrated the whole room.

That voice was one that haunted and soothed my dreams. "There's our little hero, Tom," she said. She clapped slowly three times. "He swoops in to come and save his precious love, Alicia." The voice penetrated into my eardrums, tugging at my heart. "Oh, Tom." I'd been waiting for her to say my name for so long, but not like this. Not in this way.

"I've been waiting so long for you, Tom," she told me, clicking her heels on the hard floor, closer and closer. *I've been waiting for you, too,* I wanted to tell her, but my voice was caught in my lungs, threatening to choke me. *Not like this.* Everything was wrong. I couldn't fight her.

"Angela, be a doll and throw the spotlight on him—the red one. You know I always liked *red.*" With that last word, I could hear the hunger in her voice, tinged with a laugh of a private joke that I didn't share.

CHAPTER FIFTEEN

Like a symphony filling the room with a loud syncopated chord, I was surrounded in a dark, scarlet light as the rest of the room filled with a bright, white light. Alicia sighed. "Theatrics," she confessed. "Boy, I love 'em so." I stared right through her. As if she'd peered into my head, she wore exactly what I would expect a sexy, feminine villain to wear. A light, black dress fell in a silky waterfall down her body, outlining every curve. To the left, it came halfway down her calf, but it angled upward, so the right side's end clung to a higher part of her perfect right thigh. Up at the top, it had a small strap holding it on the right side, exposing her collarbone on the right side. She had a small black pendant around her neck to lure the eye to the center of her body.

Her hair was pulled in an artistic bun, as if she were going down the red carpet. It didn't move as she made perfectly balanced steps toward me. Every click of the heels made me wince after looking at her stilettos. The heels must have been at least five inches and dangerous. They laced up her mid-calf, right up to where one side of her dress ended. They weren't coming off anytime soon. While she couldn't use them as a weapon in her hands, the way she wielded them underneath made me feel just as weary.

"Well, we all love theatrics," she continued.

I would've shot her a confused look, had I not been frozen in indecision. I didn't know if I'd have to fight, run, talk, or anything of the sort. "Who's we?" I stalled. I needed a moment to assess the situation, but, the truth was, I didn't even know what the situation was. In all reality, I was realizing that I didn't even know who Alicia was.

"Well, the vampires, of course." The words stung at me, confirming the fears in the back of my mind. I shot looks around the room, expecting a swarm of them to descend upon me and feast. I shot up and pulled the knife out, pointing it in all directions.

"Oh, honey," she said, in the cold voice she owned, "I don't need any help to kill you."

"How long?" I asked, trying to add confidence to my voice. I feared that she could hear the falter in every word. I kept my knife and my gaze pointed at her like a chain, immobile. I kicked the doll aside, giving me room to fight—or flee, if I had the option.

She watched the doll roll over, and commented, "You know, I spent a very long time on that doll, and I'd appreciate if you didn't break it." She looked at me and smiled a malicious smile. It was a beautiful smile, but it would pour ice into your soul. "I could use it for the next boy." She laughed and walked closer, clicking her heels on the floor as she did. It took every ounce of bravery I had not to stagger backward, away from her.

I didn't know why I held my ground, what it would prove, but I continued on. Maybe I knew that this was the end, and I wanted go out with pride. Maybe I thought I could reason with her, that the feelings I had before weren't a lie. Maybe I still wanted to save her.

"I've been a vampire since I was born, forty or so years ago," she finally answered, waving off the numbers with her hand like they were an annoying mosquito buzzing by her ear. "I've been leading you on since I met you three years ago," she explained, answering the question I hadn't meant to ask, but really wanted the answer to.

She stepped closer until we were close enough to kiss, or, in this case, bite, kill, stab—however she wanted to destroy me. I began to tremble, but I never let it show on my face. As scared as I was, I wanted to know. I wanted answers before I was gone. However, she didn't strike—at least, not yet. "You know," she leaned into my ear and whispered in a voice that sent a sensual, but terrifying chill down my spine, "it's too bad Jack and Hannah had to walk in on us. We could've had some real fun..." The hiss on the last word disgusted me. But, unbelievably, I grew hot under my shirt. I felt a pull to press my lips against her moist, deep red lips again, even if it might kill me.

I didn't even notice that I had leaned in until she pulled away with a satisfied smile. "You humans are so easy," she remarked. I felt a twinge of guilt at my weakness and the stab at my race. "I suppose it's not your fault. It's evolution. You humans were only built to handle, and exude, for that matter, a small amount of pheromones while we vampires were built above you. We can release enough pheromones to turn you into slaves." She turned around and created a gun with her finger. She pointed it upwards at the only window in the whole room on the ceiling. As she brought her finger down, making the motion of "pulling the trigger," there was an instantaneous crash overhead as a spray of glass came down in a shower, accompanied by a mess of seven or eight bodies, falling instantly on the floor to a loud and painful death. My mouth dropped open in horror. A few bodies twitched for a moment, but they all stayed silent until the movement stopped completely.

I could feel myself shake as I accused, "How could you?"

She turned back to me and winked. She continued to smile as she responded, "It's easy. Get a bunch of men addicted and tell them to jump through the window at my cue." She winked as she sent the "cue" right through my chest. She moaned a bit with pleasure before she continued, "So, do you want to die now, or do you want play first?" The sparkle in her eye glinted with malice.

"Why?" I asked. "Why do you want to kill me so bad?"

"Why can't you be more fun? Theatrics, my dear boy. We vampires are all wired the same. We always want everyone to end up hurt, and we want everything crazy. We all want to make a scene. All of this setup is just for you." She gestured around at the lights, the bodies, and the doll. "But, you know, there are probably a thousand scenarios playing out just like this. We vampires are all the same. We fight less than you humans when we all think alike. But, you're not anything special. You're just another notch in another one of our belts."

"Why now?" I wanted to keep asking questions, trying to figure a way out, but I knew that if I ran, she'd catch me, even in the high heels.

"Well, for two reasons. First, I needed you." I'd recovered enough thought to finally give her a questioning look. "That movie, hoax, whatever, was exactly what I needed to get us out in the open. I'm tired of hiding away. We have evolved past you, and we deserve our rightful place at the top of the food chain. And, my desire, as one of the oldest, and one of the first naturally born, vampires, I deserve the spot at the top. Not only of the vampires, but of you pathetic humans, too." She spat on the floor, as if even acknowledging that we were once above her left a dirty taste in her mouth.

I cringed, expecting her to take her disgust out on me, especially judging by the expression she held in my direction, but she didn't. She waited for me. I don't know what she was waiting for, but I had to keep her talking. "Wh-what's the other reason?" I asked, beginning to shake again.

"I wanted you to love me," she said. I choked on my breath. Before I could ask why, she pressed on. "We vampires don't feel the love you humans feel—not that we miss it at all. However, we do miss the drama it brings. How you, a weak boy caught in the middle of a storm, both in reality and metaphorically, would risk your life to save some girl—some girl who tortured you, ignored you, *destroyed you*."

She took a purposeful step toward me, stomping her foot. "Love makes you stupid. Love makes you weak. Love will kill you all one day, and it's going to kill you today."

"No," said the voice of an angel. "Love will save him today."

On the right of the stage, the same entrance I came through, stood Hannah, wet, dirty, but beautiful. She took a step forward. "Love gives you the strength to face an army, vampire or human." She took more steps. "Love gives you a reason to press on through the storm. Love helps you think clearly and follow the clues ahead, if you know where they lead." She kept walking, making every step a dagger into everything Alicia said.

Hannah made it over to me, holding something behind her back. She took my hand in hers, and said, as loud as she could muster, "Love gives you the will to do something that you always told yourself you would never do—like shoot a gun." With the last sentence, she pulled out a gun and aimed it directly at Alicia's chest.

Alicia bellowed out a laugh, and Hannah squeezed her eyes shut when she pulled the trigger. The shot rang in my ears and drowned out anything else I could have been thinking. The bullet flew straight, right into her cold, unfeeling heart. Her chest jerked backwards as the impact hit. Everything stopped as I looked forward. Alicia held the same face she had when I first met her, like she was determined not to notice the gun that just shot her.

After quite a few seconds, she looked down at the wound in her chest, and I was surprised at its lack of bleeding. She looked back up at us, her face both furious and questioning. "Are you done?" she asked, her patience apparently had abruptly run out. Hannah and I staggered backward in sync, both of us tripping over the damn doll. Hannah quickly aimed the gun again, this time at Alicia's head, but Alicia swiftly kicked it with her hard shoes before she could pull the trigger again. I watched it as it flew as fast as a bullet itself, straight into a wall, creating a crater.

I held the knife out more forcefully toward

her. She didn't laugh at me this time. "Tom, I'm done playing games," she growled. She kicked my knife as well, but I didn't watch it this time. My heart screamed at me to think of something before it was forced to stop beating. I kicked the doll in front of me at her legs, and before I had even made a decision, I was already swiftly running straight back to the dressing rooms with Hannah in tow. My leg burned and threatened to stop, but I wouldn't allow it. I didn't look back, or bear to think of what came next, I just ran.

As soon as I pulled through the curtain, Alicia was already standing at the other end of the hallway. The clothes rack was on the floor and the clothes littered the hallway. Her arms were folded across her chest and she tapped her foot impatiently. The sound of her heels emulated the ticking end of the clocks of our lives. I remembered the open door to the woman's dressing room, and, without looking, I pushed Hannah through the door, myself behind her. I slammed the door shut.

Alicia didn't try for the door immediately, so I took the chance to shove a chair in front of the door. I knew it wouldn't stop her, but those precious seconds could save our lives.

I quickly scanned the room for something, anything that could be used as a weapon. I found a pile of discarded clothes on top of what held the shape of another gun. Although I knew I couldn't protect her, I thrust another clothing rack in front of Hannah and the gun. "Use it," I murmured at her through the bright clothes.

The door burst open, shooting the chair against the left wall, breaking it into millions of splinters. Alicia stood there, calm and amused.

"Wrong choice, honey." She paused again and didn't attack, but she blocked our only entrance out. This was our last stand, and I had to make it count. She took her sweet time preparing for our end. She looked around the room and grabbed a bottle of perfume on the counter, looked at it like she was fascinated. "Hm, vanilla." She smelled it a bit and sprayed it on. Then, she burst the bottle in her hands like a white dandelion. The sweet smell of vanilla wound its way around the room, into my nose, but it couldn't tear me from the sight in front of me. After watching all of the pieces fall to the floor, she brought her gaze back to me, and said, "I guess you're next."

I sucked in a deep breath and braced for the worst, but, this time, I didn't tremble. I was here, strong, making it farther than I could've thought possible. I could buy time with my death, and maybe Hannah could be saved. I could be a hero—a real hero—one last time.

Alicia strode over to me, obviously enjoying the fear she thought I had. Sure, I was afraid, but it was blocked out by my pride. She grabbed my arm, probably to rip it off. I stood strong and willed myself not to feel the pain that was soon to come. All of a sudden, behind me, a venting sound began, but I didn't dare take my eyes off of Alicia. Her eyes, however, fell to the sound. "Seriously?" she asked what must have been Hannah.

I left her back there with a hairdryer. I couldn't believe that I'd been so stupid as to mistake a damn hairdryer for a gun in a time like this. We were both dead. But Hannah didn't give up. I could hear her advance with the heat. I felt the heat gain on my right arm as she blew the air against it. My only thought was that we were finished, obliterated. I could barely stand to think that mine and Hannah's last stand would be here, in a girl's dressing room, with our only fight consisting of hot air blowing on Alicia's cold, lifeless arm.

I continued to stare at Alicia's face. She still held a confident smile, but she didn't move. Her eyes locked on me, but began to falter on the increasing heat on her hand. I could feel her hand grow uncomfortable as it fidgeted, but I couldn't risk looking at it. I kept my gaze firmly on Alicia, calculating her next move. After quite a few agonizingly slow minutes, it never came. Her smile had begun to quiver, and I took a chance to look at her arm, wishing beyond divine hope that something was saving us. The hand was locked firmly on my arm, but it was moving. It wasn't moving from her muscles, but her skin was bubbling.

It looked as if little worms were skittering around underneath her skin, eventually bursting out and leaving only a black, charred residue. Her hand's heat grew to an intensity that set my forearm aflame with pain. When the heat became too much to bear, I quickly jerked away, straight into the makeup counter, which sent a shooting sting up my spine, starting at the small of my back. Alicia didn't lash out after me, as I had anticipated. She simply looked at her arm, eyes wide with fear. Everyone in the room stared at the scarring skin, quickly becoming dark flames, engulfing the entire limb.

The heat was so terrible; I knew I would get a second degree burn from standing so close, but I didn't have time to think about that now. Alicia fell to the ground, wriggling around, trying to put out the flames, but to no avail. She screamed the terrible roar of a beast as she continued to wrench on the ground. Hannah pulled me to her, shaking. I didn't move. I only looked straight at the woman who was trying to kill us; the woman who, up until tonight, I'd had a mad crush on; the woman who looked so human.

Eventually, the jerking stopped, and Alicia was still. Her arm was entirely gone, and the area where it adjoined was blackened and grotesque. It even singed a small part of the dress, revealing even more skin, both burnt and flawless. The floor was littered with clumps of destroyed smoking flesh, glittered with black and grey ashes.

I looked around the room and took one step toward the door. Immediately, Alicia began to breathe again, and we froze. She slowly got up, every ounce of a smile wiped clean off of her face. Her eyes were as dark and as furious as the flames that threatened her moments ago. She set her sights directly on Hannah, without fail or distraction.

"You bitch," she said in a furious, cold voice. She lunged at Hannah, pinning her painfully on the ground. I heard the hairdryer break as well as something that could've been one of Hannah's bones. Alicia swiped at her face with her remaining hand, emitting loud, harsh slaps. She began to emit other, more colorful sentences, but I wasn't listening. I scanned the room for anything hot. The hairdryer was broken, pieces still clutched in Hannah's hand. There were only clothes and furniture left in the room. And makeup. I didn't ponder or calculate; I just took a bottle of something on the counter and thrust it at Alicia's head. It was glass and shattered upon impact.

"You are really starting to piss me off," she sneered, stopping the beating on a whimpering Hannah, but not fully turning around. The bottle had emptied its contents completely on her head. I staggered backwards, fumbling around my pockets for anything else to help me. In my right pocket, my hand enclosed upon something, and I had an idea. I used my left arm to grab another bottle from the counter, and held it in a position to throw. The second Alicia turned to me, I chucked it at her face. She let out a short growl of a dog and stormed in my direction.

I tensed up, ready for my plan to fail. I needed her close—close enough to snap my neck if she pleased—but I needed a second, just one second. She strode over, looking ready to deliver the final blow. To my amazement, and my luck, she came right up to my face to say, "I'm going to enjoy this."

"What?" I asked. "Hell?" She paid no attention, but during our short quips, I set the lighter my dad gave me to the tip of her hair and set it alight. Combined with the toxic chemicals lining her hair, she quickly was consumed by the dark, dark flames. The heat was unbearable, singeing the eyebrows right of my face, and I'm sure the hair on my head as well. Alicia thrust herself to the floor again, but I knew that it would do no good. Hannah had been smart enough to move herself to the corner as soon as Alicia had gotten up.

The flammable liquids in the makeup were a catalyst to Alicia's demise. Within seconds, her head was completely covered in the fire, slowly spreading down her body. She screamed low and loud, making a sound I'd never heard in my life. It was dark and eerie—sounding inhuman and it almost made me see shadows coming from her mouth. She continued it until the fire made its way to her throat, destroying the maker.

It wasn't long before her entire body was a

large, black mess of thrashing flesh. She rolled into a chair and set it aflame as well, in turn, setting the rest of the room up in fire. I knew we had to get out of there. Even if Alicia was dying, her fire could still kill us. I took one last look back before Hannah and I ran from the room. Alicia's body became still, without flames, only a dark, ashy mess. It was unrecognizable as a human, or otherwise, body. But I didn't have time to stare at it. The room was quickly filling itself with red-hot flames. That image burned itself into my mind. I knew what had been there before. Or, I thought I knew.

I grabbed Hannah by the hand and threw her out the door.

CHAPTER SIXTEEN

We ran as fast as we could. My body pleaded for me to stop, but I knew I couldn't. I had to get out, and I had to get Hannah out. I could feel every sharp hit of pain with every step growing worse and worse. I feared that it would be irreparable damage, and I could never walk again, but that didn't matter now. We needed to stay alive tonight. We'd worry about tomorrow after the sun rose again.

Her hand was warm in mine, and I could feel her pulse in her palm. It beat just as hard and as fast as mine. I didn't know how the flames of a vampire's death worked, but they quickly engulfed the school, running along behind us, trying to finish the job that Alicia started. Somewhere, a fire alarm went off, but it stopped quickly. I assumed it was because it burned up. Luckily, it triggered all of the other alarms, and I was sure they couldn't all burn up so easily.

The alarms made way for the sprinklers which showered us with freezing cold water that threatened to kill us itself. I looked behind us for only a second and saw that the fire had no intention of slowing down. I picked up the pace, pulling Hannah forward until we reached a door. I didn't recognize it, but I wished, and I hoped that it was an exit. I didn't know how we'd fare in the storm when we got out, but I didn't have time to think. I only had time to go.

I thrust through the door and was greeted by the sweetest, most wonderful cold I'd ever felt. I was pelted with snow and I welcomed it as I ran forward and threw myself into a snow bank.

"We're alive!" I cried out.

Hannah jumped on top of me and kissed me. "We're alive!" she repeated. I kissed her back, running my hands through her knotted and singed hair. It was now time to take hold of every moment, and make the best of it.

We kissed and we kissed until I saw a red light flashing on Hannah's face. I hadn't noticed the snow letting up a little bit, into just a powder. I sat up and looked around to find fire trucks, police cars, and other cars all around the school, still up in flame.

"Kids! Are you okay?" I heard a man yell. I looked in the direction of the voice, and I saw a tall police officer running towards us.

"Yes!" I yelled back with a smile. It felt amazing. I wanted to tell the whole world that I was okay—that we were okay.

He came up to us and said, "What

happened?"

"Vampires," I answered. "What else would it be?" I doubted anybody thought of anything else these days.

"You're Tom Grant, aren't you?" he said.

"Yes, I am," I replied.

"And isn't that a vampire?" he asked, slowly pulling out his gun and pointing it at Hannah.

I quickly put myself in-between him and Hannah. "No, no!" I screamed. I sighed; it was finally time to tell the truth. "The first video...was a fake."

He didn't move his gun. "Why? So, the vampires aren't real?" He eyed me very carefully. He obviously hadn't seen any of the vampires himself.

"No, they're real," I explained. "The first one I made, that Hannah starred in, was fake. I just wanted to be famous, and I didn't know any of this would happen. Everything after my video was real. I just fought a vampire in there."

"Someone we knew," Hannah piped in.

"Someone we thought we knew," I said sadly.

He began to relax a little, but he didn't move his gun from our bodies. "Does CNN know it's a fake?"

I nodded. I was getting so tired of lying. I was getting tired of everything: running, fighting, talking, breathing.

"Why would they do that?" he inquired.

"Ratings," I told him.

That convinced him. He put his gun away and said, "I'm sorry. This has been a long week, as I can tell you know." He gestured at our unkempt appearance. "Come on, we've got an ambulance here. We can get you guys fixed up. Then, you can tell us the truth—starting with the video."

I nodded. This was the end—the real end. I stood up from the snow and immediately fell to the ground. I looked at my leg, and it was in bad shape. The wound from my knife was red, black, and orange. It looked really bad.

"What happened?" the police officer exclaimed. "Did you get bit?"

"No, no. I stabbed myself with a knife."

"Let me look at it." He got very close and said, "Come on. I'll carry you to the ambulance."

The police officer took me in his arms, and I thought about my dad, and where he was right now. Not too long ago, I thought we were the only ones left in town, but then we found Hannah. Now, the police officer and the firemen and, soon, the paramedics were all here. Our little town didn't seem so empty anymore.

EPILOGUE

The perky show host smiled as the crowd laughed at her lame joke, just because they were supposed to. The smile had become a bit awkward in the times. She worried a lot lately. Three months ago, the world had been turned upside-down and dangerous. While she felt it was her duty to remain happy and show the world that they could still live their lives, it was much harder now. Everyone could see it, and she even revealed it in some interviews.

Guests were a lot harder to come by now. Celebrities holed up in their homes, hired trained guards, and rested dormant for who knows how long. The new guest, Tom, was the one who was pointed at as the catalyst of the entire Red War, as it was now being called. Some called it the Blood War, but the government would never use such frightening terms. She introduced her guest and allowed him on stage. He limped up to his chair, with a cane to support himself. He almost looked like a young veteran, as some believed him to be.

Tom had become quite a celebrity in his own right, which he'd always wanted. He received quite a bit of mail, both love and hate, he was asked to be on talk shows, like this one, and his movie was shown around the world. At first, the fame was a bit hard and surprising, but he learned to live in the limelight and wave at the crowd.

"So, Tom, all you and your friends did was make a movie for fun, right?" the talk show host asked after a short series of introductories, and a showing of the video.

Tom fidgeted in his chair a bit, not wanting to alienate himself from this crowd. He had gotten quite good at it, but it still made him uncomfortable. "Well, actually, we wanted to get it on the news and make people believe," he answered. The few people who hadn't heard the story let out a little gasp. Tom pressed on, "Yes, we wanted to trick the general public, but we never imagined that anything like this could happen. We didn't even really expect anyone to believe it. We only hoped."

"It was made so well, right guys?" she asked the audience, trying to keep the mood light. "What's next? Werewolves? Witches?" She laughed and Tom gave an awkward little chuckle as well.

"No, actually, I was approached by the military to join," he answered. "I mean, who hasn't been approached by the military these days? But, they were at my door at six A.M. on the morning of my eighteenth birthday, because of my extensive experience with the vampires' destruction. It's weird; they want me to create a training program, starting with an introductory video."

The talk show host pondered him for a moment. She inquired, "Wasn't the video fake? And contains the wrong information? What experience do you have?"

Tom squirmed in his chair a bit more. This was the first time he had revealed his plans, and also the first time somebody asked about the story of Alicia. He took a large breath and began to explain. "Well, we had four people in our group: me, the director; Hannah, the 'vampire'; Jack, the victim; and Alicia. Alicia gathered the little things to help me edit, and was there to be a brains of the operation, besides me of course. I, I eventually realized, was just a pawn in her little scheme..." Tom let the entire story rush out of his mouth, in every detail. He had rehearsed the story a thousand times before he came on the show, but telling it was entirely different.

He added little details to his repertoire, removing dumb little things that didn't need to be there. He even went into how he had felt for Alicia before, which he never expected to reveal, but it fell out of his open mouth like water. "...but the worst part, however, was looking back on her burnt body. I thought to myself, I knew that girl. I went to school with her. I kissed her. I don't regret how it ended, but they look so human, and it's easy to get attached to them. They act human, and a few months ago, they were probably here in the audience." There was a bit of a murmur in the audience, but Tom was only making them think about what they already knew.

New technology could detect infiltrating vampires, but there was always a bit of emotion on edge, and technology could only do so much. The talk show host, not letting any worry betray her face, continued on, still trying to keep the mood light. "So, now it's you and Hannah, huh?" she asked.

He chuckled, a little more comfortably. "Well, yes. We were just dumb teenagers a few months ago, dating each others' best friends, but we realized in the end that we were all each other wanted. We've been traveling together all this time, and we plan to work on the training for the Crimson Hunters together."

"The Crimson Hunters," she repeated. "It sounds so fancy...so movie."

"I suppose it does," Tom agreed. "But, with the Navy, the National Guard, and every other branch, I'm sure they felt fancy at the time."

"Is it true that they're reverting to bows and arrows?" she asked on the edge of her seat, leaning over her desk.

In an official tone, he said, "I'm sorry ma'am, but that is a military secret." He paused and laughed. "Just kidding. Yes, they are—sort of. They're more like cracked-up crossbows. They're much faster than back in the day, but the real difference is that they can hold different chemicals that can spur fires and heat." He turned to the audience. "Always keep a lighter on you. Heat is the only known way to stop or kill a vampire."

The talk show host pulled out a glittery pink lighter. "You can even get a cool, flashy one to compare to your friends. And, hold off on getting that new phone, rumor has it that the new iPhone will be able to make flame with the new iFlame app. Or, maybe it will just be easier to overheat, as if it could get any easier."

The audience laughed again. As soon as it quieted down, she rolled to the end of the segment. "Well Tom, thanks for being the last stop on your trip. I know you're tired and have a lot of work ahead of you."

"Yep, the production starts tomorrow. If you guys want to see it, join the Crimson Hunters. We need people to fight for humanity."

ACKNOWLEDGEMENT

I have so many people to thank for this novel. First of all, I must thank 48HrBooks for helping me make my dream a reality. Next, I thank my partner, Garrett, and my sister, LeahAnn, for helping me photograph and design my book cover, which was the most enjoyable part—directly after writing the story, of course. I must thank those two again, along with Wes, Annette, Angela, Ashley, Karlee, Bek, Caty, Sarah, and Kirsten, for reading part of or the entire novel, and giving me the positive feedback I wanted to hear. I put special thanks for Jessie, Peter, and Marsha for helping me edit and catch typos and look forward to their genius in future books. I would also like to thank Jenny and Mark for creating the greatest café and wine bar I have ever worked at—as a barista and an author, along with the great people at Noodles & Company for providing me with the necessary career to fund my writing genius. I send my thanks to Scott Westerfeld, Stephenie Meyer, and Richelle Mead for writing such engaging books, inspiring me to write my own, and to Fall Out Boy, Secondhand Serenade, Paramore, Owl City, and Christina Perri for providing the background music. I put in small thanks for my dad, Rachel, Tommy, and Alyssa for supporting me through the battle, even if they never read a word. Finally, I put fifty percent of my thanks with my mother. She is currently the only person to read the entire first draft of this novel, back when it was 35,000 words. She coached me through every step, developing every character with me and exposing their flaws. She read every version, and I thank her, as this novel would have never made it without her.

In 2023, I have so many more people to think for helping me on my journey and rediscovering Scarlet Spotlight for republication. I just want to give a quick shout-out to Celeste and my library crew for the energy for the new version.

ABOUT THE AUTHOR

J. X. Burros

J.X. is an American author living in Minneapolis.
He currently lives with his husband and cat, and
he works at a local library